WAIT UNTIL TWILIGHT

WAIT UNTIL TWILIGHT

A NOVEL

Sang Pak

HARPER

NEW YORK • LONDON • TORONTO • SYDNEY

HARPER

HarperCollins books may be purchased for educational, business, or sales promotional use. For information please write: Special Markets Department, HarperCollins Publishers, 10 East 53rd Street, New York, NY 10022.

FIRST EDITION

Designed by Claudia Martinez

Library of Congress Cataloging-in-Publication Data is available upon request.

ISBN 978-0-06-173295-9

09 10 11 12 13   OV/RRD   10 9 8 7 6 5 4 3 2 1

WAIT UNTIL TWILIGHT

CHAPTER 1

THE SUN SITS FLAT AGAINST THE BLUE SKY like someone pressed it on there with a giant thumb. The day's half over, but it happens to be Saturday so we're free. David and I are walking down the crooked sidewalk, kicking up dust and stepping over cracks and fissures. There aren't many cars or houses this way, so sometimes we walk on the yellow line in the middle of the warm black top. We stop to throw some rocks at an abandoned filling station sitting in a big empty lot of weeds and kudzu before continuing our journey. The satchel with the video camera's bouncing off my left hip.

"What's with the suit and tie?" David asks me.

"It's been a year since, you know . . . my mom . . ."

"Aw, crap, that's right. I'm sorry, man."

"It's okay. We just had a little ceremony. I'm completely over it."

"Did Jim show?"

"No, he said he was busy with school. But he just didn't want to come."
I point up past the jagged tree line in the distance. "Look at that."

"What is it?" David puts his hands up to shield his eyes from the sun and follows my straight-as-an-arrow finger into the blue sky.

"There's a hawk."

"Where?"

"See, it's coming back around from those trees."

"Sure it's not a buzzard?"

"Yeah, you can tell by the V shape in the wings. It's good luck. At least that's what the Native Americans say."

We watch it make larger and larger circles over us before it glides beyond the tree line. The light sweat on our necks is cooled by a light spring breeze that smells like honeysuckle mixed with the rotten smell of the dead opossum we passed by a while back. "We're almost there," he says.

We keep walking until we finally reach a poor residential area in the backwoods on the southern end of the county line. There's a street sign at the corner that reads Underwood. It's surrounded by a cloud of swarming gnats.

"I've never been to this part of town before," I say. I take off my jacket and wrap the sleeves around my waist. I'm starting to really sweat.

"Me neither."

The houses here are all faded and old looking. Trees and bushes run amok in between and behind the houses. It's as if the houses have grown out of the woods like tumors. Some look abandoned, just ramshackle relics where you might find a squatter or stray cats. The cars sitting in front yards and alongside the road have the same broken-down look about them: rusted and forgotten. An old husk of a Chevy truck sits on four cinder blocks amid weeds and tires. A dark Cutlass lies with its rims sinking into the ground like a legless skeleton.

"Are you scared?" David asks ominously, with a smile. The smudge right above his lips is really a thin little brown mustache he's been trying to grow. He's lanky like me, but he's got a big rectangular head that makes him look a little bigger than he really is.

"Scared of what? Bring on the bogeyman."

"Who said anything about the bogeyman? Ogres are what I heard."

"Ogres, bogeymen . . . I don't care as long as I got something for this damn video project. I plan on getting an A+ in that class."

We keep walking along the shoulder of the road lined with cigarette butts and discarded fast-food containers, passing broken-down houses and empty lots. In a front yard a bony-looking old man is burning trash, stinking up the whole neighborhood with bad smoke. He doesn't wave as we go by. He just stares at us with dull eyes for a second before turning back to his fire.

"What's his problem," says David.

"Just keep walking."

We walk past a big pile of scrap metal and rust buckets to a house where a couple of middle-school-looking kids in dirty torn jeans and sneakers are hitting a Wiffle ball with a plastic yellow bat in a small fenced-in yard. The smaller, freckled face one of the two scrambles for a ball hit in our direction. "Where you guys goin'?" he asks when he sees us walking by. He's wearing a grass-stained Panama Jack T-shirt. I haven't seen one of those in years.

"Nowhere," David says.

"You're not going up that hill, are you? Because if you are, be careful on your way up," he warns us.

"Shut up, Dusty," yells the bigger kid who's wiping his face with the bottom of his shirt. He looks like an older version of Dusty. He swings the plastic bat against the ground a few times, *fwap fwap*!

"What I do? I'm just sayin' . . ."

"And there's no reason to say it."

"Say what?" I ask.

"There're some aliens in that house. They're real aliens," says Dusty.

"I'm gonna tell Momma you spooking strangers," says the older one.

"What are they, Mexican?" I ask.

"Nah, they're not right. Not human."

"Where are these aliens now?" David asks.

Dusty points to a house up the way. "You see them at your own risk." Somewhere in the neighborhood a dog starts barking, then squawks like someone kicked it.

"Would you throw the ball?" Dusty goes back to hitting the Wiffle ball with his brother. I have the urge to join in, but I got a school project to finish, whether I like it or not.

"See, I told you," says David. "Are you scared now?"

"You're enjoying this, aren't you?"

"Yes, I am."

We walk up a small hill until we finally get to the house. It's washed out and gray, with a white porch surrounded by shrubs and crabgrass. The white paint's all chipped away from the porch, and the swing that used to be there's been replaced by a moldy old burgundy couch. But the roof looks like it's been newly reshingled. The screwed-up thing is, it's almost as if I've seen it somewhere else, maybe in some bad horror movie. That doesn't seem likely though, because I don't even watch horror movies. They give me the heebie-jeebies. It's more like I've seen it in a long forgotten nightmare—forgotten but still there somewhere. We walk up to the front porch and stand there listening for any signs of life. The house looks empty and very dark. I can see some toys on the hardwood floor through the screen of the door. I hear a buzzing at my ear and slap at a mosquito on the side of my neck.

There's a splotch of blood on the palm of my hand. A half dozen or so hover around our heads.

"Hurry, before we get eaten up," I say.

David knocks. After a minute he knocks again and says, "Hello? Hello? Anyone in there?"

"I'll be right there," says a woman's voice, and then a large dark figure appears behind the screen door.

"Mrs. Greenan?" asks David.

"Yes?" she says.

"I'm David. David Mabry."

"Are you the young man that wanted to look at my little ones?" says the woman's voice.

"Yes, ma'am. Me and Samuel here, we're the tenth-graders from Central of Sugweepo High."

"Oh, is that so?"

"Yes, ma'am. Samuel here's gotta project to do, and my mom told me about you. She knew your sister back when she lived in Mobile."

"Well, if she's a friend of Margaret . . ." The door opens all the way, and I get a clear look at the dark, imposing figure. She's about the biggest woman I've ever seen. Not fat, mind you . . . just tall and big as a lumberjack. But she has a real pretty face, innocent like a Kewpie doll. It doesn't make sense at all—that head on that body.

"You boys want some sweet tea?"

"That'd really hit the spot," says David.

"I'll pass," I say.

We followed her into the kitchen.

"Sure you don't want a glass?" she asks me.

"I'm okay."

"All right, then," she says, and pours out a glass for David and one for herself. "Summer's not too far away by the feel of it. Bet you boys are looking forward to that."

"Vacation's what I'm thinking about," says David, and drinks down his glass.

"You were thirsty. Well, come on. They're out in back," she says, wiping her hands on a towel. "You can take some pictures if you want. No flashes. It scares them."

"Could I use your bathroom?" I ask.

"Sure. The one down here's backed up. Can't afford no plumber. Go upstairs and it's the first door on your left. We'll be in the back. Just holler if you can't find us."

Mrs. Greenan and David go out back and I head for the stairs. I stop at the bottom of the staircase and look up first. It's really dark up there. Almost pitch-black. It almost doesn't seem natural how dark it is, like looking into a deep hole in the ground, except up. Then I think I see something. It looks like an outline of a face peaking from behind the edge of the wall up there, but it's too dark to see clearly. Just to be sure, I say, "Hello? Anybody there?"

There's no answer. I just keep staring up there, with my hand gripping the banister, and the longer I stand there, the more frozen I feel. As my eyes adjust to the darkness, it gets to where not only do I see the outline of a face, but I see the whites of two eyes glaring down on me.

"Hello," I say again. "Somebody there . . . are you there?"

I can feel my heart thudding against my chest. Forget the bathroom, I just want to escape, but I can't move. Like if I do, whatever's up there is going to get me. Minutes pass. It feels like an hour. I think I'm going to pee in my pants. Then I hear a floorboard creak. Out of the darkness those glaring eyes blink. That's when I begin to back away slowly from the stairs. As I do, I look down at my hand, where I feel something crawling. A hairy little spider's scuttling up my arm. I swat it away and head back the way David and Mrs. Greenan went, down the dark corridor following the light to the back of the house. Once I get out onto the screened-in back porch where David is, I feel relieved. Then I hear murmuring and whispering from behind me. I turn around and nearly scream. There's another burgundy sofa where three little things lie side by side wearing blue flannel pajamas. At first I think they're mechanical dolls, but the way they're squirming and moving around is too natural to be fake. Their heads are way too big, and their arms and legs are all different lengths. Some long, some just stumps with little fingernails stuck in a semicircle. Even their eyes are different sizes, one larger than the other, and their twisted little noses are hardly there. It's like seeing them through the bottom of a Coke bottle, making everything misshapen. The strangest things are their mouths. They're the only things on their faces that look normal, and because of that they look so perfect compared to everything else on them. And those lips are moving like they're talking but nothing's coming out. Then a door slams upstairs real loud, almost angry. I can hear someone upstairs stomping around in what sounds like heavy work boots. It isn't until David puts his hand on my shoulder that I realize I'm standing and staring.

"You okay?" he asks.

"What do you mean?"

"Man, you're shaking."

He's right. I can feel my body, and it's like cold electricity in my insides vibrating me like an electric razor. "Yeah." I nod. "I'm okay." But I'm not. I can hardly even look at those things without feeling faint. Everything gets kind of dark, and my blood feels like it's cold. "I've never seen anything like it. It's like some horror movie."

"Keep it cool, man," he whispers, and nods back toward the kitchen, where Mrs. Greenan's coming. "Ready with the camera?" He seems calm like everything's normal.

"Here, you do it," I take out the digital camera from my satchel and prep it. "All you got to do is press this button to record. It should focus on its own."

"Are you sure?"

"Yeah, yeah, absolutely. Here, take it. I . . . I'll ask the mother some questions." Mrs. Greenan's leaning against the open doorsill watching me with a suspicious eye. Maybe it's the sweat beading up on my forehead. I can hear more stomping around upstairs. Then I hear a toilet flush and then a door slam real loud again. It sounds like someone's punching the side of the house with an iron fist.

"What's wrong with them?" I ask with a wavering voice.

"There's nothing *wrong* with them. They're my babies. Joseph, Moses, and Noah. They're my miracles. There's nothing wrong with a miracle, is there?"

I walk to the edge of the porch and look out into the backyard with my arms folded. I can't stand the sight of them to be honest. I think I'm going to puke but I hold it back.

"Miracles? What do you mean by that?" asks David.

"They were immaculately concepted."

"You mean there was no father."

"I guess you could say God was the daddy."

"God, huh?" David says.

"Don't they appear as miracles to you?"

"I don't know, ma'am. I can't say I've ever personally witnessed a miracle, but they don't look like normal babies, that's for sure."

"Sure they don't. They're not. Doctor told me some of what they got, but I couldn't understand what the hell he was saying. Neuro mumbo jumbo something or other. All he knew was that they couldn't change a thing and that the rest was left to God."

"Shouldn't you find out what they have? Right, Samuel? Samuel?"

"She's right," I say, looking out at the backyard. "It doesn't matter. That's just the way they are."

"You damn straight. Those doctors still, they still wanted to take them. They wanted to study them like rats or something. Microscopes . . . needles . . . X-rays . . . I told them hell no!"

When she yells "hell no," one of those things squeals, "Eeeeek!" Each time I thought I'd vomit I was able to hold it down. But I knew if I turned around to ask to use the bathroom again, I'd lose my puke-blocking focus. So I gingerly walk off the screen porch and proceed to vomit the chili burgers David and I had just had at the Dairy Queen down the road. I make sure to bend over so as not to soil my Sunday suit. David stops filming and comes over.

"I'm okay," I say before he can say anything.

"You sure don't look okay."

"I've seen this before," says Mrs. Greenan. "Can't even stand the sight of them. Time for you two to go."

"C'mon, man."

"Okay."

"Well, go on then. Go on out the back way. You don't have to look at 'em ever again. Should have known. You're the same."

David helps me back around to the front, where I take some deep breaths. "Man, what the hell just happened to you?" he asks.

"I don't know. I freaked out," I said. "I wanted something cool for my video project, not that!"

"That wasn't cool?"

"Cool? That was cool?"

"Sure."

"I wanted artistic cool, about an intriguing-life-story-in-the-South cool, not batboy-in-the-*National Enquirer* cool," I say, while taking off my tie.

"I guess it's true what they say. There are monster babies around these parts." David raises his hands zombie-style and stumbles forward.

"Let's get out of here." We walk back to the Dairy Queen, where we had left his maroon Cavalier convertible parked. I get in the passenger seat and lay my head back. "Shit, I should have gone with my dad," I say.

"Where'd your dad go?" He rolls the sleeves of his blue T-shirt up to his shoulders and lights a cigarette, letting his free arm dangle out the window.

I roll my sleeves up to my elbows. "After the service he wanted to take me out for lunch."

"Why didn't you say so? We could've come any time."

"I needed to finish this video project. I was desperate. But not that desperate." I sit back up. "What the hell were you thinking?"

"You said something strange or interesting. Pretty strange, no?"

"Would you just drive?" David takes us out of Underwood into the countryside, over the small wooden bridge spanning the narrowest part of the swamp, North toward downtown Sugweepo. It's a pretty quiet town, not much excitement, a lot of the small-town blues. I look at the name of our town on a sign with an arrow and remember reading a description in the AAA guide:

> Two hours west of Atlanta and two hours east of Birmingham, Sugweepo straddles the border of Georgia and Alabama. Population of 200,000, its main sources of income include a small college, the West Georgian, and Eastwire, a large wire-making plant.

"WHAT'RE YOU GONNA DO ABOUT your project?" David asks.

"I'll figure something out." With the spring air coming in through the windows and the slight smell of honeysuckle and wisteria, I begin to feel normal once more. Normal. I miss feeling normal.

"You goin' out to the mall tonight?"

"I'll stay home with my dad."

DAVID PULLS INTO MY SUBDIVISION and down past all the houses. My house is up on the left. After I get out of the car David says, "Hey, I didn't know it'd freak you out like that."

"You're not the only one. I'll see you at school." I go inside, and Dad's out of his Sunday clothes watching a Braves baseball game. He's aged a lot this past year. More wrinkly, more gray hairs on a slightly balding head, a little hunched over but still sturdy. I immediately feel guilty for ditching lunch, so I decide to make it up to him. "How'd it go?" he asks from the couch, his Sunday sweatpants and sweatshirt already on.

"I just saw something. Something I never want to see again. I don't want to even think about it."

"Sounds pretty awful." He smiles. "Did you get an idea for your video thingy?"

"No, I don't think so."

"You goin' out tonight?"

"No, no."

"Good, I got some steaks we can put on the grill. Get out of that monkey suit and watch some of this game. We're up three-one."

THE NEXT MORNING I GO TO CHURCH, something I started doing regularly after Mom died. It's funny—I started and Dad stopped, which I can kind of understand. I go to remember and he doesn't to forget. There were times when she managed to get us all to go, but Dad usually just let Jim and me sleep in. Though I loved sleeping in on Sunday morn-ings, I always felt a little guilty knowing Mom wanted us all to go. I can't say I really believe in anything at all, but I go for her sake now. I know she'd like it if I went, and it's a good time to let my mind wander. That morning I try to think of another idea for my video project. Seeing as how there's less than a month of school left, and Robert, my ex-partner, has forsaken me to work on his waterfall film with his evil twin, I need one quick. Those strange little babies still sit around the edge of my memory, but it isn't like a real memory, more like something I had seen on television or a movie. Nothing to see here, move on, I think to myself, and instead start paying attention to the goings-on when the singing of the hymns begins. What amazes me is how you could take a bunch of people who don't necessarily believe in anything and have them sing these hymns together and it sounds so good. It doesn't matter whether they believe or not. It's the song that's pretty, not them or what they do outside of this church. I even sing, though my singing voice isn't so good. In fact, it's terrible, but it's like I'm singing in place of my mom. It makes me feel closer to her, somehow. We sing a rendition of "Upon the Vision of the Holy Trinity," and then the preacher gives a short sermon ending with an invocation of the Holy Ghost.

With an idea for a video project seemingly a million miles away, I drive home. I got a cherry-colored Tempo that was handed down from my brother Jim, who went off to the local college, the West Georgian. After I park in our driveway, I walk down the street, still wearing my church clothes, and play basketball with some neighborhood kids. They're all younger than me, so I just horse around with them. It's a lot easier shooting some round ball than coming up with an idea.

I ASK MR. PECK ABOUT my idea block during art class when Monday rolls around. Mr. Peck's by far my favorite teacher. He's a big burly man in his late fifties with these big muscle arms from years in the navy and time spent after school in the weight room. He wears large square plastic glasses and has long sideburns. Very old school. He doesn't talk much, but on that day he says some useful things to me. "If you think too much about it, you get all confused," Mr. Peck tells me.

"So think less?"

"That's right. You see those buzzards?" Mr. Peck points to a table of students through the glass window of his office. "All they do is talk and goof around in class. They're gonna get low grades, and they deserve it! But the opposite, trying too hard, is no good, too. Just try letting the idea come to you."

I take his advice and try not to think about it, focusing on my other classes. And then it slowly begins to work . . .

Later in the week at gym the ever-bearded Coach Gaily makes us go out onto the football field instead of letting us play basketball like usual. "You pissants need fresh air, whether you like it or not," he tells us. "C'mon! Hup hup hup!"

When we all get out there, he takes us through some calisthenic drills: deep knee bends and jumping jacks, toe touching, the whole shebang.

There's a chorus of whining from the class: "Coach, why you makin' us do this?"

"Yeah! How come we ain't shootin' hoops?"

"Aww Coach!"

"This is stupid!"

"You gonna make us do this the whole class?"

"Shut those mouths! You need it whether you like it or not," says Coach.

I notice that among the few students spread out in the bleachers, one girl's wearing this bright red shirt and eating a banana. It's my friend Melody. She's a tall coffee-skinned black girl, maybe a mulatto, but I never asked. It doesn't matter. She has male admirers of every race, origin, and ethnicity. In fact, she's one of the prettiest girls in our grade. And she's one of the smartest. I know she gets good grades. But she doesn't hang around with the other popular, pretty girls like Susie and Katy. Sometimes she hangs out with the black girls, but most of the time she's alone. Most everybody likes her, and she's nice to people and happy most of the time. I've accused her of being a lone wolf, which makes her laugh. The thing about Melody and me is that when we're at school we don't talk. We act like we hardly know each other. It's something we've never even talked about but always done from middle school. It's almost like we don't want anyone to know about our friendship because people would dirty it up with their talking and imaginings. She looks very relaxed up there, like she's perfectly safe without a care in the world. I like the way it looks, and it stays in my mind for some time.

"Keep your mouths closed and finish this, then you can do whatever you want, ants!" says Coach.

There's a unanimous, "Okay Coach!" We finish our jumping jacks and then are set free. Some kids play football, some stand around talking, and others go up to the bleachers to sit down. Right next to me Joe is telling Clay how his dad is getting him a dumbbell set from Kmart. Joe's a crazy kid one grade ahead of us. He's just in our PE class because of time conflicts in his schedule. They keep talking about some of the protein and amino-acid supplements they're taking. Susie and Debbie, two of the popular, pretty blondes in our class, stand next to me sharing a Dr Pepper with Will Young. Will's like six feet four inches tall, with long blond hair and, when he's not swimming on the swim team or playing bass in a local rock band, he's usually smoking weed. Will comes over and grabs for their soda, but Susie jerks it from him. Sensing danger, I jump out of the way, and the can flies behind me. Luckily, hardly any of it comes out of the can. Will runs over to it and picks it up off the ground. After a quick examination he dusts it off and has a long drink.

"Eww!" say the girls.

I begin to walk away, looking for a pickup football game, when I hear a fizzing sound and then feel something sprinkling on my back. Will's shaken the can up and is splattering it on me.

"What are you doing, Will?" says Debbie.

He's laughing like it's some funny joke. I come up to him and push him in the chest. He just tries to splatter me again before running away, laughing his ass off. I run after him but eventually give up. It's just going to piss me off more, and he's really fast. I go up to the locker rooms to change T-shirts. Brad's in there, toweling off from a workout with a few upperclassmen. Brad's a big guy with longish red hair whom I've known, along with Will, since elementary school. He has hopes of being groomed into the starting quarterback of the football team one day. He's definitely the jock of us three, having already made the varsity football team and become a letterman. But he's a little bit of a nerd, too. I don't know anyone who's read any more books than him. "What're you doin' in here?" he asks. I show him my soda-splattered shirt, and he smiles.

"How the hell am I friends with that guy?" I ask.

"I've asked myself the same question. I think it's because we've known him too long now to break free. Don't fight it."

"Maybe that's it." I open up my locker across from Brad's and pull out a white T-shirt. "So what, now that you're varsity football you can just skip class and get all pumped up?"

He lowers his voice and whispers, "It pays to be a dumb jock, man." Then he laughs. "You should go out for varsity basketball."

"I got to keep my straight A's, and there's my SATs. Anyways, I just don't feel like it." I head for the sink to rinse out my T-shirt.

"Hey!" yells Brad.

"What?"

"Tell David I got someone who needs a small loan."

"Now you're in on his loan-sharking scheme?"

"Five percent for each person."

"Yeah, whatever." I rinse out my T-shirt and hang it up in my locker before going back out to the football field.

THAT NIGHT AN IDEA COMES to me in a dream . . .

I'm shooting my short film for Mr. Peck's art class. But it isn't a film shoot. It's a war. I'm the leader of a small band of warriors who are fighting a revolution against a tyrant dictator and his large army. A group of their soldiers corners some of my warriors in a field of golden wheat. Many of my men are already dead, but the few who remain are brave. They keep fighting in the face of insurmountable odds. The problem is, they're wearing red shirts, which make them too easy to see. So I tell them to duck down under the tall wheat blades so they can't be seen. They follow my orders and disappear into the wheat. There's this huge machine gun right outside of the wheat field that has been killing many of my warriors. It's helmed by the enemy general, a man resembling Will, with a Fu Manchu mustache. Out of frustration and fear of having all my warriors killed, I bum-rush the main gun and cover it with a black tarp, which somehow magically turns it into a video camera. Instead of killing my warriors, it's filming them. But when I look in the camera, it's those deformed babies wriggling toward me . . .

And I wake up.

THE NEXT DAY I TELL Mr. Peck about the dream, sans the babies at the end. He tells me, "I read one time about a scientist trying to figure out a formula but failing for two years. Then one night the answer came to him in a dream. Looks like the same thing happened to you but a heck of a lot earlier. Work on it and see what you find." So that entire week I focus on trying to get my idea together. I write down my dream in detail and recruit the school drama club to help. They sure as hell like the idea of being in a short film. Getting all the props is the hardest part. Army fatigues and fake machetes for the tyrants and soldiers, red sweatshirts for the revolutionaries, not to mention a big fake gun. With the help of David and Will we drive our cars with the drama students out to a wheat field I found a few hours southwest of Sugweepo. There I shoot the whole thing on handheld video. I get them to act out the scene in my dream with the soldiers looking for the red-sweatshirted warriors, while the general with the fake Fu Manchu mustache stays back with his big fake gun. We shoot for the entire day, and then when it's all over, I take everyone out for pizza.

After we finish, I go over to Will's house. I'd left a few old tapes from my handheld there in his basement when I made use of their DVD burner. Will's older brother is down there painting all the walls white. Leaning against a dry white wall are stacks of his Monet-type Impressionist paintings.

"The tapes are on the desk over there," he says. "I peaked at some of the footage. Looks good."

"Thanks."

"What's up with those baby things at the beginning of the second tape?"

"What do you mean baby things?"

"Those three freaky babies on the sofa."

"Ah, that. I don't know. I think David shot that. Pretty weird, huh?"

"Yeah, they looked so real. I don't see how they did it."

"Me, neither." Just the thought of them makes me nauseous and creeped out. I grab the tapes and go back up to the kitchen, where I fix myself a hot dog, hoping to settle my stomach. I walk outside with my food. Will and his parents are standing around in their pebble-strewn garden next to where they park their cars.

"How've you been, Samuel?"

"Good, Miss Williamson. Just busy with school."

"How's that film coming along?"

"Almost finished. I'll have to see what there's to see in the editing room."

Will's big brother comes out of the house with a shotgun and an easel. "I'm goin' huntin'. Anybody wanna come along?"

"No thanks, I'm tired," says Will. He does look tired. "I think I might be coming down with something."

"Will, you get inside and get some rest. We don't need two sick boys walking around here," says his mom.

"I don't feel sick anymore. I'm too good to be sick," boasts Will's big brother, and then he walks into the woods alone to paint one of his pastoral paintings. I finish my hot dog and go home. I never did ask him why he took that shotgun with him. Maybe he really was going hunting.

I SKIP TWO DAYS OF school and stay on the art class computer trying to make the video I shot look like the dream. Editing is the easy part because I can do it alone and on my own time. All I have to do is cut and paste. The problem is it doesn't look right. It looks too plain. It isn't until I remember those Impressionist paintings sitting in Will's basement that I can fix the problem. I manipulate the colors of the video using a program on the computer to make them look as if they're water-colored. It deepens everything and gives it the dreamy look I want. The blue of the sky bleeds into the yellow of the sun and wheat.

The red of the shirts the rebels are wearing show out like blood. It's like everything has its own aura. Most of the running time of the film consists of the machete-wielding rebels frantically running around in the wheat getting hunted down and picked off by the gun-toting soldiers. After I give the orders and the rebels duck down into the wheat to hide from the soldiers, I come running out of the wheat to cover the dictator's big gun with the black tarp. Using a little camera trickery, namely turning the camera off and then on while keeping everyone standing still, I turn the big gun into a camera, which suddenly becomes the point of view of the film. The dictator and the soldiers run, and the rebels win the battle without violence. As soon as I finish I show the ten-minute film to Mr. Peck in his office.

"Looks good."

"Thanks."

"Is this your final exam project?"

"Yeah, I think so."

"Well, just try to look busy until the end of the year, then," he tells me.

CHAPTER 2

I GET SUSPENDED BECAUSE OF THOSE TWO DAYS I skipped while
working on my video art project. And as punishment I'm put in
"lockdown" for a day. There's a trailer behind the school next to the
Dumpster for that. I get there early in the morning because if you're
late just one minute you get another day. David's already there for getting caught smoking back behind the school. All the teachers know
about the pack of cigarettes in his shirt pocket but usually don't say
anything because, though he's sixteen, David supports himself and
his mother as an auto mechanic and the occasional small-time loan
shark. He has this constant worn-out look about him. I don't think he
sleeps much.

The other two in lockdown that day are the Japanese exchange
student, Yoshi, and a skinny little black kid whose name I'm not sure
of. Once you got in there, you have to stay in your cubicle facing the

wall and keep your mouth shut the entire day. If you speak, you get another day. That's the punishment for everything: you get another day. Mrs. Smith, who I think is two hundred and two years old, sits all hunched over behind a desk at the head of the trailer, making sure we all stay quiet. Mrs. Smith's this old lady who sometimes works as a substitute teacher. She's real strict and always has a scowl on her face. I spend the morning catching up on homework and readings from the classes I've missed. When lunchtime comes, Mrs. Smith has to go get the food and bring it to us. We don't get the regular lunch. Instead, we get a brown bag of a peanut butter jelly sandwich, chips, an apple, and milk. At least we get it delivered to us, though. "No talking, no laughing, no nothing," she orders at us before she leaves to get our lunches. As soon as she goes I speak up from my cubicle.

"Hey, Yoshi. Did you really get in a fight, like everyone's saying?" I ask. I've never talked to him, but in lockdown everyone seems like a comrade.

"A black tried to throw a rock at me. So I kicked him," he says.

"Who was it?"

"He is here," Yoshi says.

"Why'd you throw a rock at him?" I say from my cubicle. There's no answer. "How long you in for?"

"One day," says David.

"Two days," says Yoshi.

After a moment of silence, "Fo'," says an unfamiliar voice from the far rear cubicle.

Mrs. Smith suddenly comes through the door and we get quiet. "Who was talking?" she asks as soon as she comes in. No one says anything. "I heard talking." There's only silence. "In about three seconds, depending on a turn of events, you'll either get more lockdown or back to business as usual."

"Why?"

"Who said that?"

"Why are you such a Nazi?" I say from my cubicle.

"Whut? Who said that?"

I stand up. "We didn't do anything to you. So what if we exchanged a few words? What do you expect? My God, even prisoners can talk."

"I want to know who talked," she says.

"It was me. I talked."

"You just earned yourself another day, mister."

"Good for you."

"Keep talking and you'll get more."

"I love it here. It's nice and quiet so I can get my studying done. I even get my lunch delivered by a Nazi." She looks at me with this look of utter horror on her face, like I slapped her or something, and then walks out. The heads of everyone slowly come up over their cubicle walls.

"You crazy!" says the black kid. I'm not sure if he means it as a question or a general statement. I head for the door.

"Where will you go?" asks Yoshi.

"I don't know, but I think she's bringing reinforcements. And I really want to get the hell out of here," I say. This must be the exhilaration convicts get when they break out because it does feel damn good.

"It looks like it's going to be that kind of day," says David, who stalks out, taking out a cigarette.

"You crazy, too. You gonna get us all in trouble," says the black kid.

"I was just gonna go outside for a smoke, man," says David.

"Everyone goes, then I go, too," says Yoshi. I'm already out of the trailer when Yoshi comes hopping out with his spiky black hair. He smiles and stretches out his arms into a Y and then takes a deep breath like he's going to start doing some stretching exercises or something. I wonder if he even knows we're getting into a heap more trouble.

With a cigarette in his mouth, David stops at the door of the trailer and looks back in. "We're an equal-opportunity breakout," he says. I hear a muffled answer from inside the trailer. "Suit yourself. You can tell them whatever you want."

Yoshi comes up to me and says, "By coming to America I miss my Japanese anime the most."

"Anime? No anime here, man," I say. "Just old Nazis and cruddy peanut butter jelly. Peanut butter jelly! Peanut butter jelly," I sing. David joins in. "Peanut butter jelly! Peanut butter jelly!" Then Yoshi, too. "Peanut butter jelly!"

It keeps going then like that until David stops us. "My house is just up the street from school. C'mon, before old Nancy Battleaxe comes back."

The black kid finally comes out with an angry look on his face. "Shoot! I feel stupid in there alone."

We all take a path through the practice field and head around the gym to the west parking lot. Once we climb over the chain-link fence at the end of the lot, we're free. Just two streets down we make a right into a suburb to David's house, which is a small duplex-style suburban home. "Come on in. Make yourself at home." He leads us into the kitchen. "I don't know about you fellas, but I'm hungry. Let's get something to eat." David cooks bacon. I fry the eggs, and the black kid toasts bread. Yoshi watches us cook and asks questions like, "You like to cook? What is your favorite food?" We're making egg and bacon sandwiches and eating them almost as fast as they're being made. When David's mom shows up, we're in the middle of our feeding frenzy.

"Hey, boys! What's this?" she asks loudly. "It's been a while since I've seen you around, Samuel." She gives me a hug. Her big boobs push up against me, and I can smell the sour alcohol breath on her. She doesn't even mention the fact that we're not at school.

"I was over here last week," I say.

She stares into my eyes with her tired brown-glazed eyes that seem to be measuring me into a shot glass. "Oh yeah, that's right. How could I forget a cute face like yours?"

"At least you look better than your head is," I say, trying to be funny.

She laughs and slaps me on the back. "I've heard that before, kid. Here, hold this for me," she says, handing me a metal flask, and then she grabs a grocery bag. It reeks of alcohol. "It's the good stuff," she says, and with that begins restocking the fridge with beer and a variety of other alcoholic beverages. She's organizing them into sections while quietly talking to herself. Along with all the alcohol she's bought a couple loaves of bread, which is funny because there's a stack of toast on the counter that the black kid has made. I get a couple slices and make another sandwich and then offer David's mother one of the wine coolers I'm drinking. She laughs. "You think I want to end up in the gutter like you fellas. Hell no." She bends over into the fridge, sticking out a large quasi-shapely butt. "Just a joke. Don't get your feelings all hurt. Just finish high school." With that she takes her drink into the living room.

After cleaning up in the kitchen, we go into David's room. "When do you gotta go in to work?" I ask David.

"Not till four thirty. I told them I was suspended and that I wouldn't get out of school till four, so I got all day." He slowly leans back in his bed and groans.

The black kid, whose name we finally find out to be Cornelius, asks Yoshi, "Why'd you come here, anyhow?"

"You mean America?"

"Yeah, I mean America."

"I came here to learn English and about American thinking. Everybody in Japan must learn English. People who speak English and understand Western culture get good jobs. I was real bad at English, but then something bad happened to me to make me study harder."

"What happened?" asks David.

"When I was in sixth grade, I living in Singapore. I sitting by a pool with my younger brother one day when a Westerner spoke to us. Unfortunately, I can't understand that much English then, so I just smile at him, though I had no idea what he saying. He kept talking, and I could sense he was getting more and more pissed off at me. I kept smiling at him, hoping it would calm him down. But no, it didn't. He blew up and suddenly grab my legs. He swung me around like it was hammer-throw event in the Olympics, you know? I ended up in the pool. I wish I learned English better then so I could respond and he wouldn't throw me in the pool. I still wonder what he was talking about."

"That's crazy," Cornelius says. "If somebody tried to do that to me and my brother, he be dead."

"Ah, he was just playing," I say. "If he was really mad, he wouldn't have thrown you in the pool."

"Yeah, us Americans like to punch when we're angry," David says with a laugh.

"Ohh! This anime was very popular in Japan five years ago!" Yoshi says. He points at the television on a dresser. There's some cartoon about robots that turned into werewolves and vampires. I've never seen it before but it looks 'crazy,' as Cornelius likes to put it. "It was first a manga—a very famous comic book in Japan. It's a video game, too."

"I thought I saw it somewhere," says Cornelius. "I played that at my cousin's. He got that game for Christmas. We played that all day."

"Oh yes, very fun. In Japan little high school girls love it!"

"High school girls? Damn!"

We spend the last hour before school officially ends lying around on the floor listening to hippy-sounding country rock and roll by a group called the Flying Burrito Brothers.

"Are you serious?" I ask when he tells us the name of the band.

"Yeah, and the slide guitarist, his name was Sneaky Pete. He invented Gumby," David says.

"Who the hell's Gumby?" ask Yoshi and Cornelius.

David looks at the two and says, "Forget it. Just listen." I'm not much into hippy-sounding rock, but it doesn't sound half bad. It's sure easy to listen to. I even nod off a couple times, it's so damn relaxing.

"Any of you ever hear of some monster babies?" I ask.

"Monster babies?" asks Yoshi.

"Yeah, some people say there're these freakish babies somewhere in Sugweepo. I heard they were out heading south, past the swamps somewhere."

"I heard about them babies. My little brother said something about that one time," says Cornelius. "He said some kids been talking about like it's real."

"They are real. I saw them," I say. "We saw them. Me and David."

"You're lyin'," says Cornelius.

"No man. We went to their house and saw them. They had these big jug heads."

"Bigger than David? Ha-ha!" says Cornelius.

"I'm serious. And their eyeballs were like . . . one big as a silver dollar and the other as small as a penny. Everything was out of whack. One arm or a leg was just a little stump with some fingernails on it and then another almost normal. The only thing one hundred percent normal were their mouths."

"Their mouths?" asks Yoshi.

"Yeah. They had these normal mouths."

"I wish I could of seen it," adds Cornelius.

"No you don't. They were nasty."

"Maybe they're not real," suggests Yoshi.

"When I first saw them I wasn't so sure myself. But the way they were squirming around . . . Jesus . . . I don't even want to think about it . . ."

"They were real, all right," adds David. "Enough to make Samuel puke."

"You puked? Damn!" says Cornelius.

"What's puke?" asks Yoshi.

"Like this, Blahhhh!" Cornelius put a finger in his mouth and fake-barfs.

"Hey hey! If you live twice, you'll never see something like that," I say. "Just be glad you didn't have to see what we saw."

"Only me and Samuel know for sure, so don't be telling everybody. Mrs. Greenan doesn't want people snooping around making rumors and all that," says David. "My mom's friends with Mrs. Greenan's sister, and I don't want any trouble."

"Yoshi can tell his friends back in Japan. They won't bother her, right?" I say.

"Yeah, Yoshi, when you go back, tell everyone about the alien babies in Sugweepo," says Cornelius. "You be a hero."

"Nobody believe me anyway."

WHEN THREE O'CLOCK COMES AROUND I sneak back into the student parking lot and drive back around to David's so I can give Yoshi and Cornelius a ride home. Cornelius doesn't live too far from David. His house is on the other side of the highway on a dirt road that I didn't even know about, even though I had driven around that area hundreds of times.

Turns out there's an entire community of low-income houses. They look kind of like shacks, with blue tin roofs and dirt front yards. And they're built directly on the ground with no real foundation, except for some cinder blocks.

"Right up there," directs Cornelius.

We pull up in front of some chicken wire that serves as a fence to a front yard of dirt. His house is like the rest of them. It seems to be built on stilts, and in the windows I can see some white eyes peering out at us from the dark. "Hey, thanks for breaking out with us," I say.

"Yeah, man, but we gonna be in some serious shit tomorrow."

"It was worth it," I say.

"Sho' was."

"Good-bye, Cornelius," says Yoshi.

"Later," Cornelius says, and then pauses. "Yo, sorry about the rock."

"No, don't worry. I've had much, much worse. Thrown in pool, remember!"

Next I take Yoshi to his host family's house. On the way I take the back roads, making sure to go through Underwood and pass by Mrs. Greenan's house. "Yoshi, that's where the babies live."

"In there?"

"Yeah, but remember, don't tell anyone except your friends back in Japan."

"Okay," he says. I slow down so he can get a good look, but I get a bad feeling, and for just a second I think I can hear a door slam from inside the place. "Looks kind of scary."

"I know." I speed up on past and take Yoshi home. I pull up the driveway to what looks like a small mansion. His host family is rich.

"Do all black people live like that?" Yoshi asks me before getting out of the car.

"No," I say. "Not all of them."

"Yes, that makes sense. Bye." On the way out I almost back into the brick-layered mailbox, which makes me nervous, like something bad's going to happen. I figure the feeling will go away once I get home, but it doesn't. And then I see it on the second shelf of my desk: the video camera and tapes stacked neatly on top of each other. I stick tape two into the video recorder and hook it up to the big television in the living room. I want to see it again. Maybe it's just sick curiosity. Maybe it's the thing that's been bothering me. I don't know. I press play and study the screen. The camera pans over the babies, then to the mother at the door, and then back to the babies. They're squirming around, moving their little arms and legs about the best they can, reaching and grabbing at things. I can see now their bug eyes are not only different sizes but different colors: blue and gray, with hardly any white, as if it was just pupil and iris. It's the same misshapen forms with the perfect mouths whispering. The video lasts only a minute or two before it stops and fades. It's something I could never even imagine, like seeing a true-to-life ghost with my own eyes. It's so creepy, yet I watch again and again before finally putting it back on the shelf. I sit there at the edge of my bed for a while. I got this cold feeling inside me. And the light in my room dims for a minute. I decide to take a nap, so I crawl under the covers for a while.

Dad doesn't get off work from the family hardware store until late that day. He's been running it since I can remember. I've spent plenty a weekend there goofing off and working the register. Since he's coming home late it gives me time to make some beef and vegetable stew. Whoever comes home first makes dinner, and that's usually me, unless we go out or get takeout. Mom was a hell of a better cook than me. That was a weird thing to adjust to when she died: not having someone who could cook. It was like, there's no food and now what? Mom must have seen this dilemma coming because when it came time for me to cook, I opened the coupon drawer, where she kept a list of recipes on a notepad, and it was all rewritten nicely in a brand-new notebook. Casseroles, stews, meat loaf, I had to learn all of it. I just followed the directions and it usually came out okay. Luckily, the stew comes out good today, and later on when Dad comes home he has two servings. I wait until he looks nice and relaxed before I tell him about skipping out on suspension. I make sure to include how Mrs. Smith was being a crow.

"She sounds pretty bad all right." He chews on a dinner roll. "Next time just keep your mouth shut and do your time. Save yourself and me some trouble, okay?"

"Yes, sir," I say.

"I want to see some A's on that report card."

"The only class there's even a chance of me getting a B in is algebra, and I don't think that's likely."

"Don't get so cocky, son. It'll bite you back in the end." After dinner Dad watches television in the living room. I'm lying in bed in my boxer shorts with the phone to my ear talking to David when Dad comes into my room.

"Have you seen Trixi?" he asks me. Trixi's a black-and-gray tabby cat we found when she was just a stray kitten meowing by the back door, hungry and dirty. At the time Dad wanted to take her to the animal shelter, but Mom wouldn't let him do it. And we raised it ever since. At least my mom, Jim, and I did. Dad always hated that cat. Couldn't stand the sight of it. He always wanted a dog. But ever since Mom died he acts like it's his favorite thing in the world. He talks to it, follows it around, gives it tuna. You'd think it was his daughter or something.

"No," I say.

"It's been a couple of days. Something might have happened."

"Cats do that all the time, Dad," I say. "They disappear for a while then show up again."

"I'm gonna go out and look for her. Do we have any chicken? She loves that chicken. Maybe I'll go out and get some chicken."

I hang up the phone and walk out into the kitchen, thinking that if Mom were here, she'd just say, "Leave it alone, George. Trixi will be okay." And that would be that. My dad takes a couple of the change jars, one filled with pennies and the other filled with nickels, and pours them out onto a table. "Maybe I'll get a live rooster and we can skin it," he jokes before leaving for the store. He comes back fifteen minutes later with some sliced chicken sandwich meat. "Come on," he says as he goes out the back door. I put on some flip-flops and follow him out back, still wearing only my boxers. He walks out to the woods behind our neighbor's house. Mrs. Heard is an old lady who lives alone. Back in her part of the woods behind her yard is a little path that I used to play around years ago when I was little. Walking out there that evening, I'm surprised how far it stretches. It goes so far as to reach some more streets and houses on the other side of the woods. I follow my dad, who has gotten way ahead of me. It isn't until I see a woman coming out of her house with the garbage that I seriously reconsider what I'm wearing.

She shakes her head and yells, "Ya should cover yourself up some before going out like that. Something bad might happen." It almost sounds like a threat.

"Yeah, I know, that's why I'm going home!" I yell back at her. I turn around and start jogging back, but I'm thinking to myself, *Lady, get a grip. I'm not naked or anything.* On my way back an old guy with a gray beard's standing outside his fence smoking a pipe, and he nods to me as I jog by in my boxers. Dad comes home thirty minutes after me without the cat. I hope it comes back, because if something were to happen to that cat, I think it'd tear my dad up pretty bad.

CHAPTER 3

AROUND THE TIME TRIXI SHOWS UP at the back door the next morning, Principal Reeves has called and told Dad everything I've already told him. As punishment for my actions I'm to be suspended for the week at home. I get the worst of it because I'm the supposed "instigator." My school assignments are to be picked up in the office early in the morning before classes start. "They're hammering down on you this time," Dad says.

"That's fine with me. I can finish a whole week's worth of assignments in a few days and have the rest of the time off. I wish they'd suspend me forever."

"That means you can help out at the store then?"

"Well . . . maybe one day."

I drive over to the school's main office after breakfast to pick up the assignments. Mrs. Janson, the secretary, is sitting behind her desk along with a couple of senior girls who assist her, you know, the pretty kind who get away with murder.

"Mr. Reeves wants to have a word with you," she tells me. I knock on his open door and peek into his office. Principal Reeves, who's talking on the phone, gestures for me to come in. He's a really big fat guy—I'm talking real unhealthy fat, with a big wart on his cheek and his thinning hair slicked to one side. He keeps saying, "We'll do that. We'll do that," into the phone. After a few minutes he hangs up and gets to lecturing me.

"I know you're a good student, Samuel. You're a smart kid, I know that. All the teachers know that. We all like you. But you can't talk back like that. Everything else you do we can live with . . . but not the talking back. That's disrespecting a teacher. It doesn't look good, you see?"

"Yes, sir."

"No matter what, these teachers have to get respect from the students. Even Mrs. Smith. I know what she's like but she's still a teacher here at Central of Sugweepo."

"Yes, sir."

"Just let it go back to the way it was before. That's all I'm saying. Back to the way it was before."

"Yes, sir," I say. "I think Yoshi and Cornelius are gonna need rides home. They both take the bus, but they don't get out till four."

"Who?"

"They were in lockdown with me."

"I don't want you seeing those boys for the rest of the week. At least not on school grounds. After a week you can take 'em wherever you want."

"Yes, sir."

I take my assignments and leave. By the time I get home I expect Dad to be gone already. But he's still there standing in the driveway talking to Mrs. Baker, who lives across the street. My mom and her were kind of friends. She's a good-looking, middle-aged woman with brown curly hair who always wears low-neckline clothes that show off her cleavage and skirts that give a nice view of her legs. She's kind of short like my mom was but has a nice figure, much better than David's mom's. I have to confess, I've imagined having sex with her a whole bunch of times. Naturally, there're plenty of girls at school I've imagined having sex with, teachers even, but when a nice-looking woman lives right across the street from you, a neighbor, it's hard to beat that. Sometimes I found her kind of annoying, the way she asked Mom to lunch or movies even when Mom was sick and tired. Mom said she was kind of needy that way.

"So here's the troublemaker," she says when I get out of my Ford Tempo. She looks me up and down. "Your father tells me you got in some trouble at school."

"I was provoked."

"I'll be sure not to provoke you."

"Mrs. Baker, I'm sure Samuel will help you as much as he can. I've got to go open up the store." Dad takes off, leaving me with Mrs. Baker, who just stands there for a while. "Your dad tells me you've got a computer and printer you make use of," she says.

"Yeah, sometimes."

"I got one, too, but the printer is in repair. I need about ten pages printed and was wondering if you could do it for me."

"Sure, just e-mail it to me," I say.

"I got the disk at my house. I'll just give it to you."

"It'd be easier if you just e-mailed it and I'll bring over the papers."

"It won't take a second."

I walk across the street over to her house and meet her partner, this brunette woman who's attractive but not as attractive as Mrs.

Baker. They have a small, makeshift office in the house. She hands me a mini Zip disk.

"There's a file called Test_1."

"One copy?" I ask.

"Yes, and if you could check the grammar and spelling, that would be great."

"It'll be a lot faster if you use grammar and spell check. I can print it out for you though," I say flatly. I can tell they're annoyed at my answer, but Mrs. Baker puts on a happy face. I don't mind because I'm annoyed at them for asking me to do their work for them.

"Okay, just print it then. How about I buy you lunch for this?"

"You don't have to do that."

"I want to. After you bring the papers we can go."

"I don't know if I can make it today," I say. "I've got a busy schedule."

"Give us your number, then. I'll call you and we can set something up later." On their wall is a little white board with some markers in the tray. I take a marker and write down my number on the board. Then I go straight home and print up their document. As soon as it's printed I place it along with the Zip disk in a manila envelope and put it on their front doorstep. I crawl back into bed.

THE RINGING OF MY CELL phone wakes me up. It's Mrs. Baker wanting to take me out for lunch. She seems hell-bent on taking me, so I tell her fine, let's do it today so as to get it out of the way. Since I'm awake I get up and study some algebra, which isn't that bad. Once the formulas and techniques get memorized, it's just a matter of plugging in the numbers without screwing up, which is the hard part. But history and biology, it's just memorizing tons of facts. I just have to dig in.

Mrs. Baker picks me up around noon and drives toward town. "I hardly ever see you these days," she says. "Not since your mom . . . I'm sorry. I didn't mean to be so casual."

"It's okay," I say. "I'm fine with it."

"That's good. Just like your mom. Sensible. You know you look an awful lot like her. I don't mean you look like a girl or anything."

"I know what you mean."

"She was a good friend to me."

"I thought we were getting lunch," I say as she pulls into the parking lot of the bowling alley.

"You've never eaten here?"

"It's a bowling alley."

"I know, but the food's good, too. Me and your mother ate lunch here sometimes."

At the entrance Mrs. Baker hands the cashier at the counter a card with a bar code on it. The cashier scans the card, and there's a buzzing sound. We walk through some turnstiles and get a seat at a table at the front next to some large windows. Behind the registers and down the way I can see the actual bowling alley through the corridor. I can hear balls rolling down alleys and pins getting hit with a loud *crack!*

I order a turkey club sandwich, and Mrs. Baker a salad. She lays her red handbag in the middle of the table after taking something out of it. "I gotta go to the restroom. Could you watch this for me?" Then she walks off.

I sit there looking out the window, getting hungrier and hungrier. The boredom of sitting there makes it worse. In the meantime her purse has tipped over to where I can see inside of it. With my finger I lift the top edge of the opening and have a look around. I can see at the very bottom some wrappers and a bunch of little chocolate candies in there. There's no way she'll know if I take one. I put my hand in and bring out a candy. My mom sometimes would give me candies just like it. She must have been getting them from Mrs. Baker. I put it back in the bag. Mrs. Baker comes back and sits down. "How old are you, Samuel?"

"Sixteen."

"Wow, you must be having some fun."

"No, ma'am."

"You don't have to 'ma'am' me. I'm your neighbor. My name is Betty."

"Betty Baker?" I said with a smile, then realized how that sounded.

"It's okay. Yes, Betty Baker, but Betty to my friends."

"All right . . . Betty."

"Thanks for the copy. We had a deadline, and the printer died last night. We're still a small operation, so we did fine with one printer, but we're going to get another so this doesn't happen."

"What do you guys do?"

"We're a small Christian publishing company."

Oh no, not a Jesus freak. As I'm thinking, this thin, stubbly-faced man wearing a tight black T-shirt sitting at a table behind Betty waves at me. I look at him and follow his line of sight to the large plate-glass window to the outside, where there's an even thinner well-dressed black man looking in. He's got a flattop that stands about an inch above his head. He waves back to the stubbly-faced white guy and goes to the front entrance, where he's stopped by the cashier at the counter. The white stubbly-faced man yells to the cashier, "He's with me!" There's a loud buzz, and the black man goes through the turnstile and over to the white guy. Within minutes they begin arguing loudly about the black man being late all the time and the white man being sick of it. The black man then says, "Is this about getting revenge?"

And then the white man says, "No, it's about you being a bitch and not giving a shit about anyone else!"

"Who're you calling a bitch?" Their argument escalates to where they're bumping chests and pointing fingers in each other's faces. It's just two guys fronting each other, but still, I can't help thinking one of them might take out a knife or start choking the other. I don't know why I'm thinking that, but I do. I get a cold, nervous feeling like when I was at Mrs. Greenan's house. The light even seems to turn down, the same way it does when clouds cover the sun. And then a weird thought pops in my head: *Those babies of hers are better off dead.* In a place where there's no pain, no worry, no loss. That's it right there. You don't lose anything, not even your mom because you never had one in the first place. Better yet, not even born. *What's the point of coming into the world like that?*

It's like in the back of my mind this is what I really thought from the first moment I saw them, but I didn't want to think it. And I hate the way it makes me feel. Like there's something not right with me thinking that. It's just not something normal people think, people at school, my friends, family . . . it just doesn't fit.

Mrs. Baker looks back to me and smiles. She's been turned around and watching the spectacle along with everyone else. They seem to find it amusing. I guess it is, come to think of it. They're both skinny little guys, dressed well, not too threatening at all, really. A server gets in between them, and the two settle down easily. After a minute the room lightens back up, and everything is regular. Our food comes, and I eat slowly and methodically, taking big bites out of the sandwich and stuffing my mouth full of fries. Mrs. Baker nibbles on her salad.

"You were hungry!" she says. I nod my head. "Do you have a girlfriend?" she asks me, but I'm watching the other table. The black guy has walked off and come back with a flower. The white guy looks around and grabs it and throws it down. They look around and shake hands.

Checkout Receipt

Albany Public Library Main Branch
04/30/10 01:25PM

Too late to say goodbye : a true story o
31182017700765 05/28/10

Wait until twilight : a novel /
31182018731777 05/28/10

OTAL: 2

"I don't have one," I say with a mouthful of food.

"Why not?"

I shrug my shoulders and just keep eating, but I can feel my face redden, and the more I try to make it stop the hotter it gets.

"Where's your partner?" I ask.

"Kathy had a previous appointment. Do you think she's pretty?"

"No . . . I mean, I didn't think about it. She's gotta eat lunch, too, right?"

"I think she's very pretty," says Mrs. Baker.

I continue eating with my eyes lowered until I'm finished. "Thanks for lunch . . . Betty," I say.

"My pleasure. Next time maybe I'll make something for you." We walk out into the parking lot, and the sun is really shining down hard. But it isn't super hot like it will get soon when summer comes around. I get in her big red SUV and put on my seat belt. It feels good to be full.

"Whaddya thinkin' about?" she asks.

"Nothin'," I say.

She drives me home and parks in the driveway. "Aren't you going to invite me in for a cup of coffee?" she asks me. It's the same kind of stuff she would ask my mom, getting her to do things she really didn't want to do. My mom was a lot more patient than me, though.

"Mrs. Baker. Don't talk to me like I'm my mom. I'm not my mom."

"I didn't mean it that way . . ."

"You didn't mean it that way, but that's the way it is, isn't it?" I say. "Try laying off a little." I go inside the house and wait for her to back out and go back to her place. I'm sure I hurt her feelings, and I don't like it. But I knew I had to nip her attempts at replacing my mom with me in the bud right there. I get in the Tempo and head on out. I take the back roads, just wanting to kill some time, breathe in the country air. I think about those chocolates, and I get this sick feeling as I go out over the bridge past the swamp, and after a couple of turns I find myself back in Underwood. I'm an idiot for coming back, but I can't help myself. It's this sick curiosity in my guts that brings me back here. That's the only way I can explain it to myself—sick curiosity. I park along the street in front of Mrs. Greenan's house. Looking at that gray house, I can't help but wonder what the hell it's like to live in there. I get out, walk up the way, and knock on the screen door, but no one's there. I peek through the windows, one of which is now all duct-taped up, but the drapes are closed. If they'd just repaint and take better care of the place, maybe it wouldn't look so damn sinister. At least the weather is fine. I don't feel like going back home just yet, so I take out my American history textbook from my car and sit on her front porch steps, where the rotted gray wood shows through all the white peeling paint. I'm on the chapter about slavery and the impact it had on the Civil War. It's hard to imagine there was a time like that in America. A car comes on by, but it's not Mrs. Greenan. A couple more cars pass while I'm reading. One of them, a white Dodge Charger with blue stripes along the side, slows down, so I get up, thinking it's going to stop. There's some bearded man behind the wheel looking at me through the window. I can't get a good look at his face, but before he speeds past I can see he's wearing a greasy-looking blue baseball cap. Standing there on her porch steps, I wonder for a moment if I'm doing something suspicious or even illegal, but I can't think of anything, so I sit back down. It's back to my studies.

I must have dozed off because my head is in my lap and there's some drool on my chin that I wipe away with my sleeve. My body feels so heavy leaning there against the post of the porch. Then I notice someone in front of me. I look up, but the sun's at his back, so all I can see is a giant shadow standing over me with blinding light coming from behind them. I still feel half asleep, so I wipe my eyes. Then without a word he slowly, almost leisurely, puts his hands around my neck. At first I think it's a joke and I giggle because I'm ticklish around the neck, but the grip tightens and tightens until I can't breathe. Panic starts to set in. I want to see who it is, but his face is just shadow and with the light from behind it, it's like looking at an eclipse. My hands can do nothing to the iron grip. Its strength makes me wonder if it's even human—maybe it's a statue come to life or a robot. It doesn't seem real. *So this is what it feels like to be choked to death,* I think momentarily, in the midst of my panic. Slowly the dark shape starts to blur, and I can feel I'm losing consciousness, as if I'm just falling back to sleep. It feels too easy. Too easy to die like this. *I'm going to die right now.* Shit. *God I hope this is a dream.* Then it all fades to a pitch-black silence.

"HEY, WAKE UP! WAKE UP!" Someone's shaking me. It's Mrs. Greenan standing over me. I can see her clear as day. I'm lying on my side with my textbook sprawled in front of me next to a grocery bag. I sit up and put my hands around my neck. The sun has already sunk below the treetops beyond the neighborhood. I was out for a good half hour by the looks of it. "What do you think you're doing?" she asks.

"I thought someone was choking me." I put my hand on my throat gently. Does it actually feel a little sore?

"Choking you? It was just a dream. You were asleep."

"I could have sworn . . ."

"Did you see anything?" she asks nervously. She looks around. "What did you see?"

"Nothing. I was waiting for you, ma'am." I keep rubbing my neck.

"What for? You want another peek at a horror movie? That's what you called it, didn't you?"

"I just wanted to say how sorry I was . . ."

"Well, you've said it, now you can go."

"I didn't mean any disrespect."

"I saw from the moment you saw them what was in your heart. I've seen it before. I don't need that around here. They don't need that, so take your apologies and be back home with you."

"Is there any way you'd give me another chance? No camera or anything, just me. I just want to see them."

"Get on out of here," she says, and goes inside the house with groceries in hand. She slams the door.

I go back to my car and sit down. My neck feels funny. A little sore. The power of dreams. Amazing. Mrs. Greenan's already gone in the house. I think I can see her behind the darkness of the screen door, but I'm not sure. I just want to see them. I don't know why. I just do. Probably to make me feel better about myself. She sure as hell hates me, though. I guess I can't blame her. I check my messages while massaging my neck with the other hand. There's one from David.

"Hey, Samuel. I just got up. Had to work all night at the garage and blew off school today. Give me a call."

I don't feel like going home so I start the car and drive on over to David's neighborhood. He's sitting on his front stoop drinking a beer with Cornelius.

"You guys look like crap," I say.

"Cornelius helped me at the garage last night," says David.

"Worked on all the night through," adds Cornelius. "Look at you, riding around like a free man."

"I should get suspended more often," I tell him, and sit down beside him. There's a shovel leaning against the steps. "I guess Yoshi's all alone in lockdown."

"I don't know. I'll go to school tomorrow and see how he doin'," says Cornelius.

"Are you digging a hole?" I ask.

"There's some punks roaming around the neighborhood . . . you're just in time. Look, there they are." David picks up the shovel and stands. Three skinny young black boys wearing oversize hoodies are walking down the street. One screams, "Whoaaaa-hoo!" and then barks like a dog. They start sauntering up to us through David's yard, which isn't a good idea. David walks out to meet them, shovel in hand.

"Didn't I tell you to get the hell outta here?" yells David.

"This ain't yo neighbahood chump!"

And just like that all three jump on him and then on Cornelius. I run and tackle one of them at the waist, bringing him down. I try just to keep him down and out of the fight, but he keeps moving around. He pushes me off and runs. Then I go to tackle the one fighting with Cornelius, but the other two are already running off. Cornelius is sitting down in the yard touching his lip. David's standing there holding the shovel.

"Did you get 'em with that?" I ask, pointing at the shovel.

"Yeah, but one of 'em got me." His hand is covered with blood.

"What happened?" I ask.

"One of 'em had a shank. I got one good on the side of the head, but the other one came around."

The wound looks like a little black slit about a quarter of an inch in his side, where thick blood is slowly leaking out.

"Oh shit! Let's go to the emergency room," I say.

"No, it didn't go deep."

"Man, you just got stabbed!" says Cornelius.

"I can't afford any emergency room." We follow him into the house and to the bathroom. With a bunch of cotton balls, rubbing alcohol, and Band-Aids we clean and dress the wound. I take a towel and wipe the blood away from his side. I peek under the Band-Aids and cotton, and the blood flow has already stopped and is already starting to thicken. It was a shallow cut.

"At least call the police and report that guy," I say.

"No, no cops." He gets another beer and goes back out to his stoop. He seems okay, so I sit beside him.

"You remember those monster babies you were talking about?" asks Cornelius.

"Yeah."

"I betcha they's just deformed. I have a cousin who's missin' a hand. Got stuck in a drier."

"These guys are all . . . They don't hardly look human," I say.

"Guess some ain't so lucky," says Cornelius.

"I heard that," David answers.

I leave David and Cornelius on the stoop with their beer and go home to fix dinner for Dad and me.

CHAPTER 4

THE NEXT DAY I TURN OFF MY CELL PHONE and study all morning. I break only for a tuna sandwich at noon. I don't get very far with studying after that sandwich because there's a knock at the door. I look through the front drapes and don't see any car. When I open the door, it's Melody. She looks at me and smiles through her curly black hair that hangs around her face. When she's this close to me and I can see the dark lashes and smooth skin, I'm reminded of how pretty she is. "How's it feel to be exiled?"

"Good. Now I see why you enjoy being the lone wolf."

"Shut the hell up," she laughs.

"What are you doing?" I ask her.

"What does it look like I'm doing?"

"Playing hooky."

"Just afternoon classes. I'm a good girl," she says. "It's been cleared by the office. Just an early departure so I'll still get my perfect attendance award, I'll have you know."

"A lone wolf and a Goody Two-shoes. That's a contradictory state to be in."

"This is coming from the same boy who has a car but rides his bike all over the place every chance he gets. Some people think that's crazy."

"That's why Americans are so fat. We drive everywhere."

"Yeah, I know. That's what you always say. So I decided to take your advice and . . ." she grabs my arm and pulls me out into the driveway. "Take a look," she says. "Ta da!"

I see that she's ridden a bike. "When'd you get this?" It's a refurbished red mountain bike. There's some rust here and there but still lots of miles left on it.

"Somebody asked my daddy to fix it and never showed up."

"Nice. No wonder I didn't hear you pull up."

"Let's go for a ride," she says.

"All right."

I pull my Schwinn out of the garage and catch up to her as she's already reached the blacktop. We ride down to the end of the subdivision out onto the country roads and past open fields intercut with woods and homes surrounded by large pastures. We just keep going and going. I take her through the swamp on over to Underwood. I want to tell her. I want to show her everything. But if she ever found out how I really think and feel about those things, she'd probably hate me as much as Mrs. Greenan does. Hell, David doesn't even know the whole story. No one does. Just me. I take her past Mrs. Greenan's house without saying a word. Out past Underwood, we ride slowly, taking time to talk but mainly just riding and enjoying the sun and wind in our faces. We ride farther out into the open country and eventually make it to the bridge that goes over the unfinished highway on the edge of town. Dad told me how that highway construction was pushed by state politicians so they could say they had used the taxpayer money, but it was just a waste. Locals call it the lost highway.

We pull our bikes off to the shoulder of the road and down the embankment where the foundations of the bridge and the upper half of the ridge meet. Hardly anyone comes around here. It's so quiet standing on that bridge, it feels like the world has ended and we're the last two people on earth. Melody would be a good Eve. Eve should be black, I think. I don't know about me as Adam, though. I can't imagine myself walking around naked. Melody climbs up onto the railing where a chain-link fence hangs.

"You think this is for suicides?" she asks.

"I don't think the drop would kill you. Probably for keeping people from throwing things."

"Look." She takes a chunk of concrete and tosses it over the mesh. "It doesn't work very well."

"They say this highway cost over fifty million."

"I think it is to stop suicides," she says with confidence.

I feel something wrong with me, something heavy in my chest, something in there sinking and slowly pulling me down. It's like one of these chunks of concrete. If I knew exactly what it was, I could give it to Melody and she'd dump it off the bridge and I'd be okay. Really okay, inside and out. Make it go away forever. But I don't even know what the hell it is. I climb up on the railing and look down on Melody. Her coffee-colored skin looks pale in the afternoon sunlight. It makes her look kind of like a ghost. Then the thought comes to me. Maybe we *are* ghosts. We've somehow gotten killed and don't realize it yet. But the thought isn't scary or strange. It's strangely comforting and leaves me feeling easy.

✝

AFTER HANGING OUT ON THE bridge, we sit down on the edge of the grassy slope. Down below is the highway and above that the green slope that meets the bridge and above that a tree line below pure azure sky. The occasional car passes over the bridge with a *thump thump thump*.

"It's been a year, hasn't it?" asks Melody.

"You remembered."

"Sure I did. Girls remember everything." She smiles. "I remember seeing your mom pick you up at middle school. She was pretty."

"Here, take a look at this," I say, and take a picture of my wallet.

"Ah! See, she is pretty."

"I took that picture."

"Are you serious? It looks like a professional job. Wow." Melody looks at it for a minute and gives it back. "You know if you ever wanted to talk about it . . ."

"I'm okay with it. I got over it months ago." I look straight, but I know she's looking at me from the side. "You wanna try riding on the lost highway?" I ask.

"Five more minutes," she says, so we stay there a little longer, the earth below us and the sky above.

The bike ride is smooth on the fresh gray surface of the lost highway, and it goes on like that for a long time, several miles, in fact. Toward the end of it, though, the pavement ends abruptly and becomes gravel. I try to bike over it, but my Schwinn becomes embedded in the little rocks, making it almost impossible to pedal. I have to get off and push.

"Can't you make it?" Melody asks.

"Hell no. Let's trade bikes."

"Ha!" She gets off and pushes, too. We walk until we reach an actual serviceable road running close to town. Melody has an errand that she can take care of in that area, so I follow her over some railroad tracks into a part of town I rarely go through. There're Laundromats, pawn shops, and cheap apartment complexes of brick and stone around here. As we pass a group of young black guys hanging out in front of an apartment building, one of them—a tall, muscular guy wearing an oversize basketball jersey—jogs up to us. "Who's that?" he asks Melody. He's young, our age, but I've never seen him at our school.

"A friend," she says without looking at him. He looks me over. I stop and put my hand out.

"I'm Samuel," I say.

He looks a little surprised and takes my hand. "Eric," he says to me, then turns to Melody, who's slowly riding up ahead of us, "Where you goin'?"

"The *Sugweepo Saver* office."

"You better bring me along to protect you," he says.

"I don't need your protection," she says. I'm biking slowly behind Melody, and Eric walks alongside me.

"Hey, Samuel, I'm just kidding." He smiles. "It used to be there were tough guys all along these streets and you'd have to pay *them* to protect you from *them*. You know what I mean?" He stops and heads back to his buddies but turns around once to yell, "You better hurry. It's almost three!"

Up ahead Melody stops to look at her watch and says, "Come on, Samuel, we gotta hurry up!" I catch up with her and we ride fast until we come to a small run-down office building. There's a sign up top that says THE SUGWEEPO SAVER in yellow. I use my lock to secure both our bikes against a railing alongside the street while Melody goes inside. I walk in, and there's one man sitting behind a desk watching TV without the sound on. He barely turns his head to ask, "Who's this?"

"A friend," she says while writing something on a piece of paper at his desk. He doesn't even acknowledge me and goes back to watching television. It's the ending credits of a soap opera, and then an animal documentary of some sort comes on after.

I stay quiet and watch the television, but I want to say something to show that I was with them, that I'm cool. I can't think of anything, so I just watch the TV. The animal documentary is one of those violent ones that shows predators devouring their prey. But then a strange thing happens. The prey starts attacking the predator. A gazelle attacks an alligator. And then I know it's some CGI crap. There's no way a pack of bear cubs could attack and kill a gorilla. It looks kind of disturbing, though. Bear cubs attacking? Babies attacking. I don't like it. It's bad enough those things keep popping up in my head like brain farts, but it's worse thinking about them coming after me. I feel stupid for even thinking it.

"Looks real, don't it?" asks the man.

"I thought it was until that last one."

"Yeah, they did a good job on this one. Maybe it's French."

"French, huh?" I say. *Maybe you're crazy*, I think to myself. Melody finishes writing and reaches into her back pocket for some money. She hands both to the guy.

"Will it be in the next edition?" she asks.

"Yup," he says. "Is this exactly the way your dad wants it?" He puts on some reading glasses. "Harvey's used and repaired Emporium . . ." he trails off as he reads silently.

"Just like it reads," she says. With that, we ride our bikes back onto the lost highway and all the way back to Melody's neighborhood, a working-class subdivision kind of like the one I live in. She holds my hand and smiles before she goes in. On my ride home, I have a silly feeling of chivalrous pride for having escorted her all the way back home. In the midst of my gallant thoughts I realize how much Melody has biked that day. She must have some strong-ass legs.

Dad is already home, and he's angry that I'm not. I tell him about studying all morning, but Dad's the type of guy who has to see something before he can believe it. I stay in my room and hit the books until dinner. I even take my dinner into my room and study while I eat. The roast beef's a little tough but good enough.

Afterward I want to get out of the house, so I take my bike out again at dusk and ride all the way back to Melody's, not with the intent to see her but just to pass by her house a few times. It amazes me that she lives in there. It seems so quiet and she seems so distant, yet she's so close, just yards away in that house. It's almost the same feeling I have about my mom. She's gone, but when I think about her, she somehow seems so close. I bike home as fast as I can before it gets completely dark on me. I'm pedaling through my neighborhood when the shaggy, white-and-gray dog from down the street starts following, something it always does when it sees me. It's even followed me all the way back to the house a few times. I don't like it around our cat, so I chase it off and even throw a couple rocks at it this time. "Get outta here!" I yell.

I SPEND THE NEXT COUPLE of days catching up on my school assignments. I've packed all my notebooks and textbooks and brought them home with me the day before. The goal is not only to catch up but get ahead. I keep my phone off and hole up in my room doing what I have to do. It's not until Thursday night I feel satisfied with where I am and watch television with Dad.

"If you study too hard, your eyeballs are gonna pop out of your head," says Dad. "That show you like is on, the one about those guys in the desert."

The show's called *Devil in the Desert*, about these college kids who get stuck in this deserted town in the middle of some wasteland.

Once they get there, the problem is they can't get out because their car breaks down and it's too hot to walk out during the day but at night these zombies come out. In order to get out safely they have to solve the mystery of the town while fighting off the zombies at night. I'm catching the reruns because the series had come on earlier during the year but I'd missed it.

"You haven't seen that dog around again, have you?" Dad asks me.

"No. I think I scared him away for good."

"Good."

CHAPTER 5

THAT **F**RIDAY **IS THE LAST DAY** of my suspension. There's going to be a short performance in the morning by the YAA order, which stands for the Young African Americans. I know I'm risking worse trouble by going to school to check it out, but it seems like too much fun, and I'm starting to get bored sitting around studying all day at home. So after Dad leaves for work, I put on his old white painter pants, some old white sneakers, and my brown hooded shirt. I'm thinking there's no way I get recognized in this getup. I drive over to the strip mall down from the school and park in front of the Kroger. I walk across the dewy pasture onto the school grounds. I could have gone around the school to the auditorium, but I want to see what it's like walking the halls incognito. A mixture of freedom and the fear of getting caught mix into a strange kind of excitement. I'm like a spy. A double agent. I find myself walking behind Candy Phillips, and she doesn't even know it's me. Candy's a Goth girl who wears lots of black. She isn't a complete freak, though. She's easy to talk to and real smart.

"Man, I'm always the victim of bird droppings," says Candy to Joanna, who was walking beside her. Joanna starts laughing. "No, listen, yesterday, I saw some birds resting on power lines, and I was real frustrated, so I shouted at them: 'Bring it on!' I don't know if I riled them or not, but one of them dive-bombed toward me. I tried to dodge it, but he crapped on my arm. I shouldn't have shouted at the birds, I suppose . . ."

I walk past them and head for the west exit. I'm starting to regret wearing Dad's white painter pants. The material's stiff and poofy, and I have to walk kind of bow-legged to keep it from chaffing the inside of my thighs. It makes me feel like a cowboy walking around in his underwear. Plus, they don't look very good. I would have been better off just wearing my jeans.

The performances have already begun when I get to the auditorium. I sneak around to the left and find a seat close to the front. On stage there're seven doors lined up in a row along a fake wall. And out of those doors members of the YAA order are coming out one at a time. Most of them are upperclassmen, but I recognize Devon from my grade. Then they go back in those same doors with a loud slam. Then come back out again and continue to slam the doors, creating crazy rhythms. The crowd's really getting into it. They're cheering and stomping. Who knew door slamming could be so entertaining? But from that first door slam I'm thinking about that godforsaken house and those loud angry door slams that came from the upstairs. It's like fate has it in for me. It won't let me forget. I want to go, but turning around and leaving means the danger of being seen. I don't have to wait too long, though, before the other students start getting up to leave. Apparently door slamming can take you only so far in the entertainment world. I follow them out.

One of the door slammers gets on a microphone and starts announcing, "Be sure to check out our Web site, www.I-Hot.com . . ." I'm too busy leaving to listen to the rest. That's when someone slaps my arm. It's Mrs. Easton, my platinum-blonde algebra teacher and probably the prettiest teacher in the school. She gives me a look as if to say, What are you doing here? I shake my head and keep moving until I'm out of the auditorium and then to the other side of the school heading toward the field. What kind of Web address is I-Hot? It makes me think of blueberry pancakes.

When I get home, it feels real good. It feels like I've infiltrated enemy lines and come back alive. I spend the rest of the day building a model F-16 airplane I got at the store last week. It's very relaxing sitting there at my desk gluing those pieces together. A nice breeze comes in through the window where the sun shines in. I started making models after watching my big brother, Jim, putting together some model ships and cars back when I was in middle school. He was about to start junior high. He's four years older than me, so at first he didn't trust me and I had to get my own models. But when I got older, he let me help him do bigger, more elaborate ones. After Jim left for college he used to come home on the weekends. Mom would do his laundry, and he'd sit around eating and watching television like when we were little kids. I visited him a few times, too. The West Georgian is less than an hour away, so it wasn't a big deal. But that was before Mom died. Since then he's hardly ever around and never calls, so it's almost like we don't know him. I must have seen him a total of two times since the funeral. Both times he didn't say a word about Mom, even though he was the last to see her before she stopped talking. He hardly even said a word to me. Just, "Hey, what's up?" Come to think of it, since Mom died it's like my family disappeared. She was the centerpiece of it all. She was always the one there holding it all in one piece. Once she was gone there was nothing to hold the spokes together. We all spanned out. Jim stopped coming home. I stayed in my room most of the time, and Dad buried himself in work. We just went our own ways for a while and didn't really speak for days on end. Dad and I just recently started talking like normal again, but Jim's still far away. It's almost like he died, too. I miss him just as much as I miss Mom. Maybe even more because he's still alive.

I take a break while letting some of the glue dry. In the meantime I make a big batch of spaghetti for lunch so Dad can have some for dinner. I wash it down with a glass of mango juice.

It isn't until late in the afternoon that I completely finish building the F-16, which I place on the windowsill to dry out completely. The paint and glue smell good, but I know if I stay in there I'll get a headache, so I go outside.

I'M SITTING ON THE FRONT steps thinking about those deformed babies again, picturing them in my mind like it'll help me understand something, when I feel this vibration come through my body. But it doesn't make me sick or cold in the guts. In fact, the whole neighborhood is shaking. It's the booming sound of a huge bass speaker. I can hear them coming from a mile away. David's Cavalier convertible has a speaker system that shakes the window frames of houses when it passes by. David pulls up with Will up front and Brad in the back. I hooked David up with Will and Brad a few years ago. Since then we hang out whenever we can, even though I'm probably a little closer to David than they are. "Let's go! Let's go! Let's go!" says Will.

"Go where?" I say.

"Party."

"No, thanks."

"Come on, it's Friday. We're not going until you get in." David turns up the bass even louder. The ground shakes beneath me. It feels like the apocalypse.

"Okay, okay! Just wait a goddamn minute!" I say.

I go to my room and throw on a new T-shirt. I smell my still freshly glued plane and admire its shiny newness once more before locking up the house and hopping in the backseat with Brad. We take off down the road with the bass speaker creating a vibration that goes up my gut through my neck up to the top of my head.

THE PARTY WE'RE GOING TO is way out in the country. David's heard about it through a friend of a friend who's way older than all of us. So we're thinking we're going to a college party out in the woods. The West Georgian College was known more for partying than its academics, anyhow. David heads due south in the general direction of Underwood.

"Why're we going this way?" I ask him nervously.

"Do you know any other way?" he says. We end up going way past Underwood, farther south out into the country. I'm talking red dirt roads surrounded by thick jungle-like woods. We go on like this for a while until these cars and motorcycles parked along the side of the road turn up.

"I think this is it," David says. We slowly back the car up and park. In the distance we can hear loud heavy-metal music coming out of the woods.

"Are you sure this is it?" asks Brad.

"This has got to be it. I mean, it sounds like a party, doesn't it?" says David. "And there's only one way to find out." It takes a good long walk to reach the clearing, and when we get there it's full of old people, not college old, but middle-aged old. Some of the old guys are wearing uniforms almost like the ones Boy Scouts wear, some of the others like Hells Angels. It's a weird mix, but they all look pretty tough. And a lot of them are watching us intently. On a makeshift stage is a band playing that loud heavy metal we heard from a distance. The main singer has this greasy blond mullet and beard. I will say this, he has a kind of charisma that makes watching him strum his guitar and sing entertaining. The guy is chock-full of attitude. I'm not into heavy metal but the band sounds okay at first. Then it starts sounding terrible when the three backup singers start screaming in unison. I mean, it sounds like they're singing a completely different song. The lead singer takes this time to pump his fist at the crowd, which hollers back at him. As his eyes move over the crowd he seems to stop at me and then points almost right at me for a second, screaming this line, "Blood for blood! Sin for sin! The circle of life comes round again!" before kicking back into the song. I want to leave right then and there.

"Man, look at all these old bastards," says Brad.

"I think we should go."

"Me, too," says Will, who's looking around suspiciously.

One old bearded guy in a black leather vest and sunglasses comes up behind us and puts his arms around our shoulders. "Hey fellas, what brings you way out here?" he says.

"Uh, heard about this from a friend," says David.

"A friend, huh? What kind of friend would send you guys out here?" He smiles and pats us on the shoulders.

"We should probably be getting back," says Brad.

"Noooo, noooo, stay awhile. I was just kidding. We're gonna have some fun."

We're given beers in clear plastic cups, which we politely accept. Everyone's drinking beer and smoking. We try to sneak away, but that same guy keeps stopping us and gently encourages us to stay. In the middle of a song with the guitars driving and the music really loud, the singer starts jumping around. He gets so worked up that he takes his shirt off and puts on a blue cap that he pulls from his back pocket. A mosh pit is forming at the front of the stage. Meanwhile, the singer's running around in circles with that cap on backward. I recognize that cap. It's the cap on the guy who drove by Mrs. Greenan's house when I fell asleep on her front porch. In fact, I'm sure of it. It comes back to me, how it felt like someone was strangling the life out of me, those cold hands around my neck. I was just waiting to see those babies, then something like that happens. And it feels like it's happening again right there in the field. I can feel the gripping sensation around my throat. All the while that singer's getting more and more agitated. He gets to shaking and flailing his arms about like he's having a fit. He falls back and starts squirming around, almost like he's imitating those babies. Watching him makes the choking feeling worse. I put my hands to my neck, but there's nothing there, just my own hands. Everyone else is enjoying the show. The mosh pit is swarming. Even David and the guys seem intrigued by this guy's onstage antics. I'm the only one freaking out, and it's getting to where I'm feeling dizzy and everything's spinning out of control. Then the song finally climaxes and the singer dives off the stage into the crowd, where he disappears into the sea of overflowing bodies. The song ends, and the pressure around my neck goes away. I start to look for where the singer went, but the old guy standing by us grips my shoulder.

"Where do you think you're going?" He points to the stage where a man sporting a huge beard, I mean Old Testament, Moses, ZZ Top huge, with a bandanna gets on the microphone. "It's time for the singing contest," he announces. "Each group must choose an ambassador and send them up to the stage to sing a song of their choice." A runner comes around with pieces of paper and a pencil stub for each group.

"Write down a song, Samuel," says Will.

"Why me?"

"C'mon just write something."

"Don't worry, we're not gonna get picked. Just write one."

I go ahead and write down "Lift Me Up." A runner comes by and picks up all the papers and takes them up to the stage, where the emcee starts flipping through them.

"If he calls on us, I'm running," I say.

"Okay, we'll all run," says Brad.

The emcee calls out, " 'Lift Me Up!' Who's the lucky man? Come on up and represent your group."

For a split second I think, *Samuel, you can do it. You can go up there and sing.* I try to pump myself up, but that moment of silly inspiration lasts about one second at the thought of that pointing finger and the voice singing, "Blood for blood!"

"You guys ready?" I whisper. We all nod, then sprint toward the road with our youthful legs pumping away. Some hands reach out for us along the way, but when we reach the road the only thing following us is their raucous laughter. We keep running all the way to the car and get out of there as fast as we can turn the Cavalier around.

Down the road a ways we pass a black man walking with a big wooden crate on his shoulders. "Let's give that guy a lift," I say.

"What?" says David.

"Those guys back there are nuts. If some of those guys are around, who knows?" adds Will.

"He's obviously not one of those guys."

"Never pick up hitchhikers," says Brad.

"He's not hitchhiking. Look at the size of that crate. You could fit a black bear in that thing. C'mon."

"If something happens, it's your fault," he says. We stop and go back.

"Where you goin'?" David asks as we drive alongside the old-timer.

The black man watches us suspiciously with his tired-looking red eyes. His shirt is open, revealing a bony black chest. "To ma house," he says.

"You know about those crazy bastards having a party back there?"

"I heard somethin' goin' on. None o' ma bidness."

"You shouldn't be walking around out here right now. Get in, we'll give you a ride to wherever you're going."

"It's okay, they don't bother me none."

"That thing looks heavy. Come on," I say. "We just wanna help."

He looks at us like we were crazy. I'm surprised he finally accepts. That box must have been pretty damn heavy. He puts the crate in the trunk and gets in the back with Brad and me. He smells like sweat and fish.

"You gotta helluva system in here, boy," he says.

"Yeah, I got friends that work at a car stereo shop."

"Good to have friends," he says.

He navigates us to a little house, half of which is covered in wisteria vines. When we pull up, a black lady comes out with four barefoot children behind her. It turns out that the crate he's carrying is filled with fresh fish. He's having a fish fry to commemorate the recent passing of his father.

"How's about some fresh fried fish?" he asks us, taking the box out of the trunk. We look at one another and know none of us want to stay, so we respectfully decline. He asks us to wait and goes inside. He and his woman go in, but the four children stand there watching us shyly, curiously. They look nice, healthy, normal as can be. And I think this is the way it should be. Not like Mrs. Greenan's ungodly babies. The old guy comes out with a little mason jar half full of what looks like water. He holds it up. "You boys ever tasted mountain dew?" he asks.

"All the time," says David.

"I ain't talkin' 'bout on sodie pop." He opens the jar and the smell of alcohol attacks our noses like hornets.

"Holy shit. What is that?" asks David.

"Mountain dew. The real mountain dew. Now, remember Barry when you're drinkin'. Have fun, boys."

We take the jar and head back into town. Helping that old-timer makes me feel a little less crappy about coming all the way out to the country to get harassed by a bunch of scary old perverts.

Brad's first to spot the host of colorful moving lights coming from the Kmart parking lot. It's one of those traveling fairs that pass through town once a year. Even from a distance we can see the Ferris wheel and tea cups twisting and turning. I haven't been to one of those since I was kid, but we all want to go tonight. We pull into the parking lot, and Will immediately takes out the mason jar and has a drink. His face turns into a disgusted grimace like he sucked on a lemon.

"How is it?" I ask.

"Here, see for yourself," he says.

I take a drink and it burns a trail all the way down to my stomach, bringing tears to my eyes. "Man, that's terrible," I say.

"Whoooeee! Skizzet!" says Brad after he drinks.

After a minute or two I feel it smoldering in my stomach. Strangely enough, it feels good, and I want more. It's just the taste that's the problem. Will and Brad go to buy some fountain drinks while David and I wait in the car. David takes another sip.

"Give me that," I say. It tastes just as bad as before. They come back with four orange soda fountain drinks, which we spike with the mountain dew. The soda does a good job of masking the horrible taste, and it goes down a little easier. We take our drinks into the park and buy a bunch of tickets for rides and games. The place is packed mostly with kids and their families, but there are some high school and college kids, too.

The line for the Ferris wheel isn't too long, and it looks like fun. Brad and David think it looks gay for two guys to get on together, but Will and I don't care. We give a couple tickets to the operator and get seated. The big wheel moves up each time a person is seated until Will and I are a quarter of the way to the top. Then after a moment we lurch forward, and the whole thing moans and groans as we start turning down and then come back up to the top, where we get a view of the whole town.

"Look," I say, and point at David and Brad down below. We give them our middle fingers, and they start cheering us on. The turning of the wheel and the drinking, the crazy circus music, the lights of the town, my friends' happy faces, the stars in the sky all go to my head. It feels like I might split open. After the ride's over Brad and David give it a twirl, not even caring if it looks gay.

We play all the games: shooting little metal ducks, throwing little rings onto Coke bottles, doing the strength test with the hammer, all of them. Then the guys want to get on the spinning cups, but just looking at those things spinning around makes me queasy. So I go for some water while they ride the whirling dishware. Along the way I pass by the funhouse, where a hawker is yelling, "Come one, come all, into the funhouse of amazements and horrors, ghouls and angels, through the labyrinth of mirrors and freaks . . ." The line's empty and I have some tickets left in my pocket, so I step up and give the old scummy-looking carnie a ticket and go in with my spiked orange soda drink in hand. I follow a black painted corridor until I get to a black door, which I walk through and find an array of strange body parts floating in large bottles of formaldehyde. Snakes, a heart, a brain, kidney, even a head, which I don't think is real. There's a whole corridor full of them placed on black swathed podiums of different heights. I look at them all slowly, because I'm the only one in there. One of the bottles contains a deformed fetus. It's got two big heads, one growing out of the other like it's trying to escape from its brother. It looks so real. It could just as well be one of Mrs. Greenan's alien babies floating in there. Dead. Stillborn. Not even a chance. But those alien babies are still alive, breathing, squirming around. Squirming like that singer on stage having a fit. That singer is the freak. What a creepy bastard. He belongs in the jar. I move to the end of the jars, where there's another black door. The next chamber is an assortment of cheesy relics. A little crusty-looking mummy in a coffin sits on a table. A skeleton with angelic-looking wings hangs on the wall next to a skeleton with horns. A stuffed two-headed calf and a stuffed one-eyed pig stand in a little corral full of hay. I stop a moment, taking a close look at the angel skeleton while sipping my orange drink. There's no one around, so I touch the left wing to see if it might be real. I pinch the bone, expecting it to be brittle like plaster of Paris, but what happens is the entire wing breaks off with a *snap* and falls to the floor and splits into three pieces. I think I hear someone in the previous chamber where the pickled weirdness was. "Crap," I say, and go through the next door. I freeze for a moment because there's a guy looking straight at me in the flashing corridor. Flashing because there's a bright-as-hell strobe light blinking in there, making everything look all herky-jerky, and like it's not real. When I turn to run, so does he, in that kind of broken, discontinuous way strobe lights make things look, and I realize it's me. It's a mirror that leads into a labyrinth of more mirrors. I hear the door begin to open at the back of the other end so I run into the maze and start making random turns, right and then left. I feel like a laboratory rat in a bad dream. It's hard enough to get my bearings with those mirrors making everything look like there's more depth than there really is in there, but the strobe light makes it even harder to tell where the hell I'm going. I have to keep my hand on the cold mirrors so I don't run straight into them. I get caught in a dead end and backtrack a couple turns and keep going until I stop at a strange sight. My blinking reflection is all twisted up into a two-foot-tall ball and my misshapen face a bug-eyed mask of something stupid and hateful. It's one of those distorted mirrors that bend your reflection. I step back, and my shape changes into a coiled-up snake and then back to the two-foot-tall thing. An ever-changing warping of reality, like nothing is normal, at least not for long. While I'm staring at myself, a twisted figure steps in behind me, right over my shoulder. I turn around to look behind me, but it's just another reflection on a mirror about five feet away. At least I think it's a reflection. It looks like a face smiling at me, but I can't tell for sure, what with the lights and the distorted mirror and the distance. But if it was a reflection, then how the hell is it still over my shoulder? It should be in front of me now that I'm turned around. I turn back to the front and then back again. I tell myself it's just my imagination playing tricks on me, but my heart starts to get real busy. I can feel it pounding against my rib cage. I throw my orange fountain drink at it. The cup almost looks like it's moving in slow motion because of the lights, like a stop-motion animation reel, and it splashes open against a mirror. It's just a reflection for sure, but that shapeless face is still there over my shoulder. "Fuck it," I say to myself. I take off running. There're a dozen of my reflections running alongside me in all the mirrors, but I don't see that other figure. I keep running anyway until I reach the last black door and I'm outside on the other end of the funhouse standing on black pavement. I'm back in the real world, where people are walking around having fun at this traveling carnival. The sounds of carnival music, the smells of popcorn and hot dogs, it all floods back in.

"Damn man, you look like you just saw a ghost," says Reed Callahan. He and Chip Callahan are standing there watching me catch my breath. They're guys from Sugweepo City High School, the crosstown adversaries to our Central of Sugweepo High School. We're the Central of Sugweepo White Camels, and they're the Sugweepo Trojans. Their school is twice as big as and much nicer than ours. If I had lived within the city limits, I would have probably gone to Sugweepo. Living outside city limits as I do requires a stiff tuition fee, which I know Dad can't afford, so I don't even ask. I've played against Reed on the junior-varsity basketball team. He comes off the bench like me, but when he gets in the game, the whole Sugweepo side would yell "Reeeeed!" He's the most popular guy in the tenth grade over there. Chip is his cousin, not as athletic but prettier in the face. And also more ruthless. I heard he'd go down to Florida on spring break and ride around on scooters randomly punching people. They both would have made good Nazis: blond, blue-eyed über-boys. Still, they were always cool with me when I ran into them.

"Shit," I say, and wipe the sweat off my face with my shirt. "I got a serious case of claustrophobia in there. Whew!"

"Claustrophobia? What's up with that?" Chip says. Reed and Chip are flanked by some of their cronies. They all have pretty girls with them, cheerleader types. From behind me a young couple comes out of the funhouse laughing and talking about how corny that place was. I catch my breath and realize how silly I was being in there. It was all just shadows and light.

"Hell if I know," I say. "Maybe it was the mountain dew going to my head."

"Is that what that is? I can smell it a mile away," says Chip.

"Mountain dew. Homemade by Barry," I say.

"Who's Barry?"

"Barry's a real nice guy, lives way down south. Sorry, it's all gone."

"We got our own stuff," says Chip.

"Hey, I guess I might be seeing you on the basketball court. You goin' out for varsity?" Reed asks.

"I doubt it," I say.

"Why not?"

"I just don't feel like it."

"That's cool, man. You should hang out with us sometime. Maybe play some ball."

"I'm down with that." We exchange numbers, and I walk back over to the spinning tea cups. Brad and Will are sitting on the ground looking pale. David's already puked and wiping his chin with his sleeve.

"Come on," I urge them. "We've still got to go on the rock-climbing thing."

"No more rides."

"I'm definitely gonna climb that thing," I point at the rock-climbing wall that has been set up down the way by the cotton candy machines. There're four walls ranging from kiddy all the way to expert, which is not only extremely high but has a rock face jutting out from it. That means at some point I'll have to hang off the thing without the help of my legs. I want to try it, though. I'm still all worked up from the funhouse. "Come on." There's quite a crowd around the wall, even a few local celebrities. I recognize the town mayor and a local radio guy I met once at one of our basketball games. We wade up to the front so I can give the operator my ticket. He soon has me suited up in a harness and helmet.

"Boy, you been drinking?" he asks me while suiting me up.

"No, sir," I say. "This harness works, right?"

"Just hurry it up."

The operator hooks the rope to my harness. The rope goes up and loops around a pulley at the top of the cliff and comes back down to a man holding it. Two climbers compete at a time. I'm paired up with a very fit-looking woman who has a cheering section of a husband and three little kids. It's too bad I'll have to kick her butt in front of her family. We both start off real slow. It must be her first time, too. My coordination is a little off, but once I start moving I feel okay. The truth of the matter is that the guys and I haven't drunk that much, just enough to make us feel drunker than we actually are. Once I find the grips, pulling myself up is a piece of cake. I learned from playing basketball that it's all about using your legs.

The outcropping is where it gets hard. It's all about arm strength, as you have nowhere to push with your feet. The lady falls off and screams but is caught by the rope and then lowered slowly. I start hearing some cheers.

"Keep goin', Samuel!"

"Spiderman!"

"Come on, you fuckin' monkey!"

I have to pay attention now because one misplaced grip and game over. With each successful move I grow more confident, and that confidence is magnified by my slight drunkenness. Once I work my way out from under the outcropping I climb up fast. Down below they're cheering. The operator and harness guys start yelling at me to come down. I'm supposed to ring this bell at the top and then let go, allowing the harness holder to ease me down, but I go ahead and climb all the way to the very top. On top of the cliff there's a toolbox and a bottle of water sitting on something engraved into the surface. It looks like a bird or phoenix. They're still yelling at me from down below, so I grab the bottle of water and throw water on the whole lot of them. The crowd is really getting excited. I pour the remainder of the water onto the engraving. And then for a split second I see or at least I think I see a familiar-looking blue baseball cap floating at the far end of the crowd. It disappears among the excited faces looking up at me.

"If you don't get your ass down here right now, we're calling the cops!"

"Okay, okay!" I say.

"Back up and we'll let you down!" I slowly back up, holding on tightly to the rope while looking up at the night sky with all its stars. *Hell, how many blue baseball caps are floating around out there right now?* "Don't try to climb down! Just let go! We'll catch you—don't worry about it falling."

I let go with my arms out. The crowd oohs and ahs as I slowly descend with the water on the engraving dripping down off the cliff onto my head. A couple of guys immediately grab me when I land. It's Will and Brad. They help me out of the harness. "He's with us," they say, and start pulling me along. We start running back to the parking lot. "You crazy bastard. What were you doing up there?"

"I just wanted to see," I say as we run back to the car.

Though we haven't drunk that much, and it's been over an hour since we began drinking, Will takes the wheel for David, who isn't the most reliable driver in any state. They drop me off first. I notice on my way in a big stack of long white tubes in the garage. They look at least ten feet long and wide enough to fit a softball through. Looks like Dad's going to do some plumbing work. When I go inside the house, Dad's in the living room watching television.

"Where ya been?" Dad asks.

"The traveling fair at the Kmart parking lot," I say, and go straight to the bathroom to brush my teeth and take a shower.

As I make my way from the bathroom to my bedroom, Dad asks, "How was the fair?"

I stand in the hall doorway. "The rides are for kids, you know, but it was still fun."

"Yeah, it's always like that," he says, and then adds, "The spaghetti was good."

I go to my room and check the model airplane, which is now all dry. I take it from the windowsill and carefully place it on the dresser. I go to bed early and make sure to look at the plane one more time before I close my eyes. The last thing in my mind as I settle into sleep is a blue baseball cap sitting there in the darkness of my mind.

CHAPTER 6

I GET UP EARLY SATURDAY MORNING TO HELP DAD out at the family hardware store, where my main duty is manning the register for most of the morning. It's pretty slow. I like it best when there're customers to deal with, otherwise it's pretty boring. So I read the paper from front to back and look out the store window at the passing cars. Luckily Cornelius and Yoshi pull up on a dirty old motorcycle that sounds like a lawn mower going *thump thump thump*. Cornelius is up front steering, and Yoshi's holding on behind him.

"Whose dirt bike is that?" I ask when they come in.

"Mine," says Cornelius. "Me and my cousin fixed it up."

"Cool," I say.

"You wanna ride?" asks Cornelius.

"I got to stay behind this register or my dad'll kill me. What're you guys doing?"

"Cornelius is going to show me the dirt track where everyone rides," says Yoshi.

"By the gravel pits?" I ask.

"Yeah. We wanted to see if you come, too. We all ride together."

"You think you can squeeze three people on that thing?" I ask.

"Sure, I done it before," says Cornelius.

"I don't know, man."

"This your store?" asks Yoshi.

"Yup."

Yoshi and Cornelius walk around the aisles and then come back to the counter and hang out. Dad shows up later in the morning, and I introduce Yoshi and Cornelius to him. He shakes their hands and asks Cornelius, "Is that your dirt bike out there?"

"Yes, sir."

"He fixed it up himself," I say.

"I don't see any helmets."

"We ain't got none."

Dad just shakes his head and then tells me to take a break. "You're not gonna ride that thing without a helmet," he tells me.

"I know," I say.

I take Cornelius and Yoshi around back, past the bathroom and office where there's an old emptied-out storage room. While Cornelius and Yoshi snoop around I do some light stretching and sit down on a concrete slab. It's quiet in there, real quiet and dusty, except for Yoshi and Cornelius talking about who'd win a fight between a grizzly bear and a tiger. "A tiger has claws and teeth, man," says Cornelius.

"A bear has claws, too."

"As big as a tiger?"

"Yes, I saw on a nature show . . ."

I'd like to join in on their debate, but I don't feel like it. Yoshi and Cornelius know about those babies, but they haven't seen them. Not like me. They haven't felt the way I feel about them. And those feelings just seem dark and wrong. At that moment Yoshi and Cornelius seem in a completely different world, where I'm just an occasional actor. A double agent for real. A phony. I cross my legs and lower my head. Then, in with Yoshi and Cornelius's ramblings, I think I can hear some music. It's very faint, but I recognize it immediately. It's "Moon River." A wave of memories comes flooding in . . . My mom playing this song on her old record player while Jim and I are in his room playing video games on the Atari . . . Me asking Jim if I can play, but he's too involved in playing Defender even to answer me . . . I walk out of Jim's room and when Mom sees me in the living room, she pats the seat beside her on the sofa for me to come and sit down . . . She's got a big smile on her face and a newspaper in her lap. It made me happy to see her happy. But this music I'm hearing isn't the record or even the original recording, it's too clumsy and all the instruments are wrong, not to mention Audrey Hepburn isn't singing.

"Do you hear that?" I ask.

"Hear what?" says Yoshi, who stops bouncing a small rubber ball he found on a counter.

"I can hear it, too," says Cornelius. "I thought it was a stereo or somethin'."

I get up and they follow me out the back door of the store to find a guitarist, a trumpeter, and a guy playing a recorder, performing in the empty lot behind the store. "Is that 'Moon River'?" I ask.

"Yeah, sure is," says the trumpeter.

"Sounds good," says Yoshi.

"What the hell are you?" asks Cornelius.

"We're the Abandon Mints," says the guitarist with curly brown hair and black-framed glasses.

"What are you doing playing here behind my dad's store?"

"We're practicing. We're supposed to be in the Spring Fling

Band contest at the West Georgian College. We need to practice playing out so . . . we're playing out. We just randomly chose the first spot we could find just driving around. I hope your dad doesn't mind."

"Hey, do you sell thread? I told my mom I'd get some thread for her," says the trumpeter.

"We have twine. I'm not sure about thread, though."

"Are we finished then? We've been doing this for an hour," asks the recorder player.

"I don't know? Are we?" asks the guitarist.

They all look at one another again.

"Okay then. Tomorrow at three?" says the recorder player.

They all nod and dump their instruments in the back of a station wagon parked along the road. The recorder player and the guitarist get in the car and leave while the trumpeter comes back.

"My car's parked out front," he says.

"Just follow me." I lead him, Yoshi, and Cornelius through the back into the store. I walk them to the shelf with all the twine and wire and tape. "It's for your mom, right?" I ask.

"Yeah, she wanted me to get some while I was out of the house."

"Here, just take it." All three look a little taken aback. "I hate being salesman, anyways."

"Are you sure you can do that?" he asks.

"So generous a man!" says Yoshi.

"Damn," says Cornelius.

"It's nothing. Just go out the back."

I walk him to the back, where he stops and takes out three dollars. "Here, take it, man. You should come out to the concert. It's at the college in two weeks."

"I'll think about it," I say, and take the three dollars. Once he leaves, we three go back up to the front.

"Here," I say to Dad, "I just sold a spool of twine to this musician guy I just met."

"You what?"

"There were some college guys in the back lot. They were playing music—"

"Playing music? Son, you can't just sell our stuff like that. It needs to be done up here at the register . . ."

"Uh, we should be going," says Cornelius. "Come on, Yoshi, we gotta go."

"Okay, 'bye." He waves at me, and they both head out. Dad's going to lay into me some more, but Cecilia, this red-headed lady who buys big amounts of supplies at a time, comes in to save me. She works for a bunch of contractors who get their supplies from the store.

"Samuel, you're growing up like a weed," she says when she walks in.

"Yes, ma'am," I say.

"You ready for some heavy lifting?"

"Yes, ma'am." She gives me the yellow order form, which I take to the back where we keep all the bulk items. I use the dolly to take all the boxes out to her van. Then I load them while Dad and she talk. I can overhear her talking about referring some other contractors to his store, which I'm sure Dad loves. After I load all the boxes into her white van, she tips me a five-dollar bill.

LATER ON AT LUNCH DAD doesn't mention my under-the-counter sale of the twine. He even takes us to get some steaks at a local steakhouse nearby called the El Rancho. The whole family used to go there on Sunday afternoon. Mom and Dad would pick Jim and me up from the house after church, and we'd all get the buffet and stuff ourselves. Mom would make sure we'd fill ourselves up, encouraging us to eat more and more until I thought I'd explode. It was fun, almost like an eating competition between Jim and me. These days it's just Dad and me. Jim wouldn't come anymore even when he's home.

Instead of the buffet, Dad and me both order T-bones with baked potatoes and mixed vegetables. Then we sit and wait. Across the aisle from our booth are three middle-aged black men in a heated conversation about money. The two sitting together wear nice-looking suits, the kinds with open collars without the ties. The guy across from them is bald and wears a black leather jacket.

"Did you ever find something for the video project?" Dad asks. I'm surprised because usually we don't talk much when we're eating here.

"Yeah, that's what got me that first lockdown. I skipped classes so I could finish it up."

"Oh," he says, pulling out a newspaper. "What were those kids doing back there behind the store?"

I explain to Dad how they were practicing in an open public space for an upcoming performance. He seems confused by the whole thing as I try to explain, so I change the subject to something more suited to his understanding: plumbing. "Is that what you're going to do with those pipes I saw in the garage?"

Dad gets a twinkle in his eye and leans back. "You know your mother was the creative one between us. Not me. Don't have an artistic bone in my body. I guess you might have got it from her side. Back when I first met her she was really interested in the arts, but then Jim and you came along, and next thing you know we got other things to think about." He takes a drink of sweet tea and continues. "When she found out she was sick, she spent some time on her own coming up with things. Ideas, designs just for herself. She gave me one of them. Called it a piece of installation art. Ever heard of that?"

"Sure. It's like sculpture, except you can use anything, everyday materials to fancy media stuff, whatever, to make some area feel different than before."

"Right. I figured you would. But anyhow, she gave me a design for some installation art, and I told her I'd make it come to life. Her creativity and my hands. I never got around to doing it. Made me sad just to think about it, especially after she died. I don't know, son, I just figured it was time to do it. I promised I would. Better later than never."

"What's it going to be?"

"It's hard for me to explain, and I don't really understand it myself. She called it 'art for the sake of art.' 'Something to make you feel. Feel anything you want,' she said. Just wait till I finish it, and you can see for yourself." He went back to his paper, officially ending his talk.

It was about the weirdest thing Dad has ever done. Art? Dad's right about him not being the artistic type. If anything, he was the opposite. Mom definitely had an artistic streak. She liked movies and music and books, but Dad? No way. I ponder a little bit more about this strangeness while Dad reads the paper. Then the steaks come. They're good: nice and juicy. As we eat the conversation in the adjacent booth is becoming more and more intense. They're keeping their voices low, but the two sitting together are really pissed off at the one sitting across the table from them. I'm watching them while I eat, and it looks like it's going to calm down a little when the black guy with a mustache pulls a gun out of his jacket and points it at the bald one wearing the leather jacket. Dad must have seen the gun, too, because he says, "Son, don't move, okay?"

"Okay, Dad."

"Eat your dessert."

"I don't think I can finish it."

"Just pretend to, then."

The booths are high enough to where we can't see the booths in front or behind us, just the one across the aisle. So we're the only ones who can see the gun. The man who's holding the gun is talking about being disrespected and how he isn't at all like him, the bald guy, who's got his hands up. The gunman then gets up, careful not to expose the gun, and sits down next to the bald guy. He puts the gun to his head, and I can hear the bald one silently begging, "Yo man, don't do it. I got kids." The gunman's friend on the other side seems scared, too, and is quietly talking to the gunman, telling him to chill out and put the gun away before something bad happens. I can see him out of the corner of my eye pointing the gun at his neck, his head, his guts, just all over his body to scare him even more. He keeps talking about how serious he is. "Man, you know I'm serious right?"

I get that cold dark feeling again down in my guts, and it's as if there's no sun and the light of day doesn't have a source—it's just there with no starting point. It's the kind of faint glow you see at dusk. The fork I'm holding starts to rattle against my plate, and I realize it's my left hand shaking. I put my hand below the table, where I try to calm myself by rubbing my thigh, but it won't stop trembling. I look over at the black man and then at the gun pointed at his terrified face that's contorted and twisted with fear, his eyes as big as saucers. In that instant he doesn't look human. More like a grown-up version of one of those alien babies. But those babies aren't scared, they're just deformed. Or are they? What the hell do they feel? My hand keeps shaking. Suddenly, the bald guy shouts out, "Oh!" and raises his hands as water squirts out of the gun. He wipes his face and looks at his wet hands. The guy with the gun shoots some water into his own mouth and drinks. The two wearing the nice suits start laughing.

"You think that's funny?" asks the bald guy angrily. "That ain't funny! Mothafucka!" He curses and cleans off the water with a napkin while the other two are slapping their knees and hunched over from laughing.

Dad looks at me and asks, "You ready?"

"Yeah," I say. I follow Dad out of the booth and up to the cashier, where we pay. As we walk across the parking lot to Dad's car he puts his hand on my shoulder, and I'm so tense I reflexively jerk. He doesn't say anything and keeps it there as we walk. It isn't until he pulls out of the parking lot onto the road that he says, "Son, some folk are just plain crazy and stupid. All you can do is avoid people like that, but if you have to interact with them, keep it cool, leave them behind, and forget about the whole thing ASAP."

"Okay, Dad."

He drops me off at home telling me, "Take it easy the rest of the day."

"All right," I say halfheartedly as I get out.

"I'm serious, son. Just relax," he says before leaving for the hardware store.

I LIE DOWN IN BED but can't unwind no matter how hard I try. I keep seeing that scared, bent-up face and the way it made me feel, all dark and clammy. I even start cold sweating on the bedspread, so I give up on relaxing and go out for a bike ride to try to clear my head and get some fresh air. The morning sun has been enveloped by a fluffy layer of gray clouds, but it doesn't look like rain. The wind cools me down. I keep going out farther and farther on the back-country roads, aimlessly riding around until I come upon the dirt road that cuts through the old swamp. I stop on the rickety old bridge and look out over the bog. A chorus of frog croaks rise from the surrounding tall grass. The mosquitoes start ganging up on me, so I push on to Underwood. I'm going to see Mrs. Greenan and apologize again. No matter how strange those babies are, no matter how disgusting, I want to see them again because I don't want to be afraid, and I don't want to feel the repulsion. I hate it. It just doesn't seem right for me to feel that way.

I go down the hill at the top of Underwood Street and stop at the house. Down the way that kid, Dusty, sees me from his front yard and comes running. "You came back."

"Doesn't look like anyone's home, though." But behind the screen door the main door is open. I go up and knock. "Hello? Anyone home? Mrs. Greenan?" I wait, but there's only silence. I turn back, but then I hear a high-pitched squeal, "Eeeeeek!" and the hairs on the back of my neck rise. It's one of those babies.

"Did you hear that?" asked Dusty.

"Hey, do me a favor and keep watch. I just wanna make sure they're all right."

"I wanna come in, too."

"Here, take my bike and go put it in front of your house and come right back then."

Dusty runs and takes the bike down to his house. There's some distant thunder that sounds millions of miles away. He comes back and joins me at the front door and says, "Hold on a second," and then screams at the top of his voice "Heyyaah!" into the old house. We both scamper down to the sidewalk and wait. No one comes to the door, so we go back up to the porch. Dusty holds the screen door open for me and I enter the dark foyer. It's real cool in there. What with the drapes and the lights out, it's kept out the heat. We walk into the living room. The floorboards creak. There're some sports magazines on the floor in front of the big old television. It looks as old as the brown couch and recliner that line the edge of the room. We go back into the corridor where there's an old rotary phone on a table against the wall.

"Do you smell something?" I ask him.

"Yeah."

"What is it?"

"Smells like my daddy's feet." Dusty starts heading toward the kitchen.

"Hey, where you going?"

I follow him into the kitchen. Beside the refrigerator there's a stack of old black garbage bags, but that's not the smell. "Why don't they take this trash out?" says Dusty, and then stomps on an empty soda can. The crunching sound of the can is real loud. He could ruin everything.

"Hey, if you wait outside for me like I asked earlier, I'll give you a dollar."

"Let me see it," he says suspiciously.

I take out my wallet and show him a wrinkled old dollar bill. "Tell you what. Make that two," I say.

"Okay."

"If someone comes, you holler at me," I say.

"All right." He goes back out the front. I start looking through the pantries and cupboards. There's lots of canned foods, macaroni, and cereal. Nothing weird here. I slowly make my way up the stairs, and the bad smell becomes stronger. It smells like sawdust and vinegar mixed with a dirty toilet. "This isn't any feet," I say to myself. I put my hand to my mouth and nose and keep the other on the banister. First, I check the bedrooms. All the beds are unmade. The dresser drawers are open. There're dirty clothes everywhere. The entire house feels abandoned, not at all like the way it was the first time I went in there with David. Mrs. Greenan doesn't seem like the type to keep such an unkempt home. I end up following my nose. The smell seems to be coming from a closet in one of the bedrooms. I peak in through the slats of the closet door, but it's too dark to see anything. The loud crack of thunder's getting closer, and I hear a few raindrops beginning to splatter on the house. It feels as though my heart's going to bust out of me. I take a deep breath and open the door slowly. The smell almost overwhelms me, but I stay put. My eyes are drawn to the floor, where a burlap bag lays. Something's moving in there. I don't like the looks of it, like there might be rattlesnakes in there. But I've got to look. I've got to know what the hell's going on. My body moves from without. It's like I'm watching myself kneel down and carefully untie the strap. I hold my breath as my unsteady hands open up the bag. It's them, those godforsaken babies. They're piled on top of each other. One of them turns and looks at me sideways, showing the whites of its bulging eyeballs, and yells "Eeeeek!" out of its perfectly formed mouth. I can hear the screen door slam shut from down below and then footsteps, but they aren't the steps of that kid. They're the sound of heavy thudding boots stomping around down there. I turn over on my belly and crawl under the bed, swiveling myself toward the door like a cockroach would. The man seems to be walking around and then stopping and then walking around again down below. My hopes of him leaving the house are quickly dashed when those steps begin coming up the stairs. I'm lying on my stomach with my ear to the floor, and he sounds like some giant in his castle with me the little intruder whose liable to get crushed. A loud wave of thunder rolls and shakes the house, and one of the little babies slowly comes crawling out of the closet on its belly. With its one good arm and leg, it reminds me of a wounded soldier who's been blown up and is trying to get away. Then it stops halfway to the bed, looking up at me, drooling, wide-eyed. It looks like it's whispering something to me the way its mouth is opening and closing like a fish out of water. I want it to stop. Then, the loud booming steps come into the room. I can see dirty black work boots and the bottom of some worn blue brogans frayed at the seams.

"Whaddya think you're doin'?" says a man's voice. When I hear its strong piercing tone, I feel something cold come over me. The boot pushes the baby back toward the closet. "C'mon." Then a hand comes down. The baby looks me in the eyes as it's lifted up and out of sight. "You tryin' to get away? You little demon. Get back in there. If it weren't for yer momma, you'd be dead like you should be. Miracle, my ass. Satanic piece of shit. I have every right to get rid of you. One day I will." A thud comes from the closet, and he walks back out and down the stairs. A television turns on. I wait a minute before sliding myself slowly out from under the bed and toward the window. By the looks of it I'd probably break a leg if I jump from up there. I'll have to try another room. Thunder's coming in regular intervals now, but there's hardly any rain. Just a light trickle but the drops are heavy. I gingerly tiptoe to another bedroom, one where a window overlooks the roof of the front porch, which declines enough to where I think I can jump from it without hurting myself. I try opening it, but it's jammed. If I put force into it, I just know it'll be loud. So I wait for a thunderclap to cover the sound. A white bolt of lightning flashes. A few seconds pass. Then when the rumbling comes, I push as hard as I can. There's a loud crack from the window, which opens slightly but not enough for me to slip through. I hold my breath. Footsteps are stomping up the stairs, so I frantically tiptoe behind the door. He walks past and goes into the other room.

"What the hell was that?" the man's voice says. I can hear him searching the closet. "Was that one of you fuckers? Couldn't be."

I'm really sweating. My heart feels like it's going to pop. The boots come around to the room I'm in. I hear them stomping around. A dark shadow moves across the wall. The window slams shut. "Shit," he says. I can hear him checking around the room. It gets real quiet. I can't hear a thing. Then the door I'm hiding behind is flung closed and he's standing there right in front of me, a tall man with a scruffy face, bearded and dirty, and longish dark blond hair over cold gray eyes. He's kind of lanky, but he looks strong, like he's made of steel and wires under that tight flannel shirt he's wearing.

"What the hell? Get out of there!" he screams at me.

He's pulls out a knife from the back of his jeans. It's one of those big hunting knives with the teeth toward the handle.

I immediately raise my hands. "No, please. I was just curious. I just wanted to see them. Please, I'll go and never come back. I promise. I made a mistake."

He grabs my arm and jerks me into the other room. His grip is powerful. "What'd you see?" he asks.

"Nothing. Nothing. I didn't have a chance. I got here right when you got in."

His look of rage relaxes a bit, becomes thoughtful. "Yeah, I was only gone ten minutes to get some beer. I love beer." He lowers the knife but keeps it close. A slight smirk emerges at the corner of his snarling mouth. He looks at me close. Close enough for me to see the blackheads on his nose, the moisture of what smells like beer on the lower part of his short unkempt beard. He smells like sour sweat and alcohol. I keep looking down at that knife. He reaches around and grabs my wallet. "Let's see who we got here." First he takes out the cash and counts it before putting it in his pocket. "Thirty-five-dollar finder's fee!" Then he takes out my driver's license. "Samuel Polk!" he says. "Aye, what have we got here?" He finds the picture of my mom behind my driver's license. "Whoooo! Who is this?"

"It's my mom."

"Your momma?"

"Yes, yes."

"I'd like to Samuel Polk her!" He puts it in his pocket. "I'll be keeping this for future reference."

"No, please give back my mom. You can keep the money, everything, just give that back," I start to cry.

"Oh! Oh, boo-hoo! It's just a goddamn picture." He puts my driver's license back in my wallet and tosses it to me. "You can keep that. A feller needs a driver's license. Pick up some hot chicks, right! Then Samuel Polk 'em!"

"Can I go, please?"

"Shit. I's just playin'. I know all about you. You're the one who threw up as soon as you saw . . . them." He nods his head to the other room.

He sheathes his knife somewhere behind his back and puts his arm around my shoulder. "Why didn't you say who you were? Come on. Look all you want." He leads me into the other room and grabs the burlap bag out of the closet. "Here," he says, and tosses it onto the bed, like it was a sack of potatoes. One of the babies partially pops out of the bag on impact. He grabs it brutally and it screams, "Eeeek!"

"Damn! Look at this thing. It's the ugliest thing you've ever seen, right? Disgusting, but you can't take your eyes off of it. Here, take it."

"No, I shouldn't."

"Don't worry, they're sturdy little bastards." He shakes it and it squawks, "Kyaaa!" When he stops shaking it, the baby becomes still. It keeps looking at me and at the man. Back and forth, with fear in its eyes.

"The smell," I say.

"That ain't them. It's the bag. It's my skunk bag." He hands me the baby, which I hold out from my body. He takes the burlap bag and dumps the other two babies onto the bed. "Put it down," he says, so I gently lay it beside its siblings. "Not like that," he says, and picks it up and slams it down as it squeals. "Got it, Mr. Fucking Compassion?" He pulls out his knife again and makes a cut on his own forearms. "See how sharp this knife is? See?"

I nod my head.

"Look." He puts the blade close to my face. I don't answer. I'm so scared it's like reality is starting to tear apart right before my eyes.

"Don't look at me like that. Don't look down on me, boy." He pulls back the knife and slaps me across the cheek. The tears start coming down my hot face.

"What do you want?" I yell at him, anger beginning to well up in me.

"That's the spirit!" He picks up one of the babies with his free hand and comes close to me. "Hit it." I stand there, and he says, "What are you waiting for, you little faggot!"

"Why are you doing this?"

"Isn't that why you came here?"

"No, I just wanted to see them."

"Liar, you came to kill them."

"No, I'd never."

He takes the knife and makes another cut on his own forearm. "Eeeeek. Kyuuuuu!" The baby screams. Then he makes a cut in the part of his chest that's exposed at the top of his shirt. "It's getting closer, closer. If it gets any closer, it's gonna cut him."

"Please don't do this!"

"Do what? How do you know what I'm going to do?" He looks at me squarely. "Hit or I start cutting . . . both together. All three of us will bleed. One happy family. Blood is blood. Death is life. Three for one. Thrice cuts the knife!" He stabs at my arm, grazing it.

"Oh God, stop. Please," I say. I'm crying, and I can't stop. He makes a motion to stab again. Then I slap the baby, lightly grazing its cheek.

"Eeeeek!" it says, then moves its mouth like a fish.

"Again," he says.

"No."

"Look at it. It doesn't even feel it." He presses the tip of the knife against the baby's belly. "Now hit it again."

I hit it again.

"Eeeeek!" it says. The sound of it screaming gets under my skin.

"Harder." I do as he says. "Again! Again! Again!" I'm hitting, but it's like I'm watching myself from above me, like I'm a ghost. "Good! Now choke it."

"Please stop."

"Okay, okay. You're right. This one's had enough." He drops it onto the bed and grabs another one. "This one, then. Choke this one."

"No, please. Just let me go."

"You puked the moment you saw them. They disgust you as much as they disgust me. Now you're about to disgust me, too."

"It's all a mistake! I'm not disgusted anymore!" I say.

"Liar."

He drops the baby on the bed and puts his knife back. Next thing I know, he's got me by the throat, choking the life out of me. It feels the same as that day on the front porch here. The same inhuman grip. It was him. He presses me down on the bed, and I can feel the babies next to my head. "Now see what you made me do? Now see what you made me do, you fucking piece of shit!" It feels like my head's expanding. My face feels red hot. His contorted face gets closer until it's right in front of mine, so close I can't even see it anymore. He lets go and then stands above me.

"Watch carefully," he says. And then deftly chops at the front of my throat with his forearm. I can't breathe. I grab for my throat, expecting it to be crushed. "Now watch," he says again. And a right roundhouse comes around and hits me on my left temple . . . then darkness . . . a kind of bruised ugly darkness, unable to breathe, and flashes of lightning close by in my mind's eye. I'm gone for a while. Then there's water on my face, and I'm coughing. The man is standing over me with an empty glass.

"Eeeeek!" screams one of them, lying against my head. "Eeeek!"

It's so loud. It hurts my ears. My hands start shaking, and then my whole body's shivering like it's zero degrees.

The man puts the knife up to my crotch. "I'll cut your pecker off. Now choke it."

"Eeeeek!"

"Shut it up, boy." He takes one of my trembling hands and puts it on the baby's neck.

"No," I say.

"Eeeeeek."

"We hate that noise. That stupid mindless voice! Shut it up."

"Eeeeek! Kyuuuuu!Kyuuuu!"

I start to squeeze, and it squeaks shut. My hand stops shaking.

"Good, see. Now stop for a second."

"Eeeeeek! Eeeeeek! Eeeeeek!"

"God, shut it up, boy! Shut it up! We hate it!"

He's right. I want it to shut up. I want it to be quiet. I squeeze. And its face turns red, and its malformed eyes get big like a quarter and a silver dollar. Its mouth moves silently, and I realize how much more I hate that. There's a flash of lightning, and then I feel the man behind me start to choke me. He's laughing, and soon I can't choke the baby anymore. I grab his hands and then he lets go. I fall over.

"Remember what you did here tonight. Remember how you felt. You're the one. It's you," says the man. And I feel he is absolutely right. I am as guilty as he is. I choked it, just like a murderer. I would have killed.

"Go away from here. Go back from where you came. I'll give you ten seconds. Nine . . . eight . . . seven . . . six . . ." He turns his hand and puts his arm over his eyes like he's playing hide-and-seek.

It takes a moment to register. It might be a trick. He's going to do something else. Cut me, torture another one of them, something else insane. But he doesn't. He keeps counting. Then I stand and clamber out of the room and down the stairs, sprinting out to the sidewalk and down the street, back to the yard of the boy, who's nowhere to be seen. It's raining now, and I can't tell if I'm crying or if it's just rain on my face, but I'm trying to keep from screaming. I jump on my bike and start riding as hard as I can through the smell of blood and copper in the air.

I TAKE A LONG, HOT shower, put on a new pair of jeans and the LIVE FREE OR DIE T-shirt Jim gave me for my fourteenth birthday. It's tight, but it still fits. There's a note on the fridge from Dad saying he went out to see a movie with Tommy and Red from the store. I drink one of Dad's beers but don't like the way it tastes so I pour it out into the sink. To get the taste out of my mouth, I eat some vanilla ice cream and then lie down on the couch and watch television. I just want to do everything I can to bring my reality back together again, anything to forget what I saw . . . what *I* did . . . and get back to normal. I can't let anyone know. It's too fucking horrible, all of it, including me. *Don't even think about it*, I tell myself. *It's over anyway. Keep it normal*, I say to myself. Normal. Normal. Normal. *No, don't say it too much or it sounds strange*. I doze off early in the evening and then wake up at ten o'clock at night, wide-awake, feeling better, but I really want to be around people, so I decide to take my bike out again. I don't usually ride at night, but it's cool and clear out and I want to ride under the stars. The mall is kind of far, but I want to try and catch Dad at the movie theater. Before I go, I write a note and leave it on the refrigerator just in case I miss him. I've never ridden to the mall on my bike. Mom had always forbidden it because the highway was too busy and too dangerous. She had forbidden a lot of things, like swearing, leaving the toilet bowl up, drinking beer, staying up late. Since she's gone I've done all of them. What's funny is I liked it better when I didn't do those things because she told me not to.

It turns out she's absolutely right about riding on the highway. There's tons of traffic, cars and trucks flying by me, and it takes forty-five minutes to get to the mall. In the end I make it in one piece but vow never to do it again. By the time I get there the parking lot is practically cleared out except for some kids cruising around. I don't see Dad's car. What I see are two cops standing beside their car watching me suspiciously. I ignore them as I keep riding around the parking lot looking for Dad's car, but those damn cops start shining their flashlight at me and yell at me to come over. Before I even get to them the muscular black cop's yelling in my face, "You know there's a curfew for bike riders, don't you?"

"Curfew? Why?"

"You know how dangerous it is to be riding out this late on a bike? Your bike doesn't have any lights. You don't even have a helmet. That's against the law, son."

"How should I know that?"

"Do your parents know you're out riding your bike?"

"My dad went out with some friends, so I left him a note."

"What about your mom?"

"She's dead."

The two cops look at each other, and their puffed-up chests deflate just a little. "Get in the car. We'll put your bike in the trunk and give you a ride home."

"Can't I just ride home?" I plead.

"We can't let you do that. It's for your own safety."

I get in the back while the two cops have a private discussion outside. I don't like sitting back there staring at the grill separating the front seat and the back seat—the seat where criminals sit. I call home on my cell phone. There's no answer, but I keep calling and calling. On the fifth try Dad picks up. It sounds like he just got in.

"What are you doing riding around at this time of night?" he asks me.

"I needed some fresh air, but Dad, listen—"

"You don't think it's dangerous riding around on the highway at night?"

I say, "No," and then, "Maybe. There were so many cars . . . and the exhaust . . . I can see why the ozone is falling apart."

"Where are you?"

"The mall. These two cops stopped me."

"Police? What did you do?"

"Nothing. They got me for riding my bike at night."

"What?"

"That's right."

"Tell them I'll come and get you."

"You better tell them—they probably won't listen to me." I open the door and tell the cops, "Hey! It's my dad. He said he'll come get me!"

"Let me talk to him," says the fat white one. I give him my phone. He talks for a minute and gives me back my phone. "Your dad's on his way, so just stay in the parking lot until he shows up, all right?"

Then they leave just like that, as if nothing happened. I feel much better once they're gone, but I have to admit I liked just talking to those cops. It helped me feel a part of reality again. This is real life, the sane world. What happened earlier in the day was a case of bad luck, a run-in with a nut job, and just like Dad said: deal with them, leave, and forget about it ASAP. I lock my bike up to a light pole and walk toward the movie theater. I go up the stairs toward the mezzanine, and along the way I run into Clay from school and a couple of his friends, one of whom appears to be Joe, that crazy kid from a grade above us, staggering down the walkway when the rest of us stop to talk.

One interesting thing about Joe is his nickname, "Captain Crazy." I'm not sure what he has, schizophrenia or bipolar disorder, but everyone knows he takes medication and has spent some time in an institution. Not that there's anything wrong with that. It's more the fact that he's known for jumping out of moving cars, taking craps on the floor of department stores, and getting into a ton of fights, not to mention the drinking and drugs. "Is he with you?" I ask Clay.

"Ignore him. We're ignoring him," says Clay.

The sober friend pipes up, "I can't believe we're ignoring him."

"Who wants to deal with that?" says Clay.

Joe finally realizes he has lost his two buddies and begins looking around for them.

"He looks like a zombie," I say.

They both think that's funny. "What are you doing out?" Clay asks.

"Just riding around. What about you—did you see a movie?"

"Yeah, but we had to leave because ass head over there couldn't sit still," he says.

"Where are all your women?" I ask, knowing he did well with the girls.

"I was thinking later we'd go to a party and find some. You wanna come?" he asks.

"The cops just stopped me for riding around on my bike. My dad's on his way to pick me up."

"Are you serious?"

"Holy shit," says the sober friend. "You should have told that pig to go eat a doughnut!"

"Yeah, so I gotta wait around for that."

"Good luck with that," Clay says.

"Good luck with *that*," I say, pointing to Joe, who's staggering back to them. I go up toward the theater and pass a large group of guys from Sugweepo High. The rivalry between Sugweepo and Central of Sugweepo oftentimes goes beyond mere sports and academics into a personal disliking of each other. There've been quite a few fights between the two. I play it cool and walk past. There among them I see Reed. He gives me a silent nod, and I nod back while continuing on. It's weird seeing him without his cousin Chip. It's like a grilled cheese sandwich without the cheese. Speaking of the cheese . . . out in the mezzanine where the benches are I see Chip standing over some guy with a bloody nose. There's a small crowd gathered around him.

"You took my girlfriend, you son of a bitch!" I can hear the bloodied guy say to Chip.

"Man, you deserved it."

"Bullshit. You deserve it."

An upset-looking girl sits on the bench watching them anxiously. I put my hands in my pockets and walk by. Across from the theater are several shops and restaurants. One of these shops on the second floor called the Grab Bag stays open till midnight. It's a weird store owned by a bunch of older guys who wear all black and have tattoos all over their arms. The place is pretty busy even at that time of night. I walk up the stairs to the entrance. Behind the register in the front area is a bunch of tobacco products, cigarettes of every kind, cigars, pipes, you name it. That's where most of the activity is. Toward the back of the front room it's more like a museum. There aren't many items, just ancient and strange things, old vintage lighters and license plates and jewelry. I check out the lighters and find this one that's shaped like a big black cylinder that you click at the top to make the flame come out.

"Hey, I like your T-shirt," says someone from behind me. "Yeah, you," says one of the owners. It's an older guy with long gray hair tied in a ponytail.

"Thanks," I say. "It's the New Hampshire state motto. My brother gave it to me. He says it's on every license plate."

"Look over there, boy." He points at some of the license plates on the wall. The New Hampshire license plate is smack dab in the middle. LIVE FREE OR DIE it reads, just like the back of my shirt. "Didn't I see you the other day? Maybe at a party?"

"No, that wasn't me," I say, and head for the second floor, where they sell rock-and-roll music, comic books, and coffee. It's not as busy as I thought up there, just a few people looking at the CDs and records and others standing around drinking coffee. The guy behind the counter turns out to be the guy who gave us the beer and kept us there at that field party when we wanted to leave. He doesn't look at all menacing now, more like a slightly overweight, middle-aged clerk in a comic-book store. I try to get him to look at me, but he acts like he doesn't know me. I browse a little, and then when I have the chance I ask him if they might be interested in buying my old comic books. I'd collected some when I was in middle school and have a cardboard box full of them.

"We don't buy from people. We just order the ones we want," he says.

"Okay," I say.

"Well, what do you got?" he asks me.

I tell him what I remember from the top of my head, and he has this bored look on his face until I mention the graphic novel *Son of the Demon*. His face perks up, so I ask him if I could bring them by.

"No, don't," he says.

"You don't have to buy them all, just the ones you want."

"No, we don't do that."

I decide to leave then, but the guy says, "Wait."

I just leave anyway. Shit, Dad's probably already there. I go down the stairs and out of the store and out to the parking lot and look around. It's times like these I wish he'd get a cell phone. I check my bike, and on the seat is a small envelope. Inside is a house key. I deserve it for making him come out here and not even being there. I start calling home on my cell when Dad pops out of nowhere like some ninja, wearing his old gray Members Only jacket.

"I'm sorry, Dad."

"Where were you?" he asks.

"I went into the Grab Bag, you know the store with the comics and CDs and all that."

"You were shopping?"

"No, no," and I start telling him about what happened in the store. He puts his hand on my shoulder, and I flinch.

"What happened to your neck?"

"You mean this? I . . . I went out riding my bike and ended up in this neighborhood at this house and . . ."

"And what? What happened? Who did this?"

"There were some kids from school. We got to horsing around, and one of them got me in a headlock."

"Headlock? Looks like he nearly tore your head off."

"I know. I told him if he didn't let go, I'd beat him with a stick."

"You see the car?" he asks me, pointing.

"Yeah."

"Put your bike in the back, tie the trunk down with the twine inside, and wait for me," he tells me.

"Where're you going?"

"Just wait, I'll be right back."

"Dad, you don't have to . . ." but he's not listening. I follow but then turn around and put my bike in the trunk. I almost did it. I almost told him. But I couldn't. I was an accomplice to all of it. Hell, it was all my fault. I should have never gone to that house in the first place, let alone kept going back like I did. It was so stupid. I screwed up big time. Dad comes back a little later, and we start for home.

"What happened?" I ask him.

"Stop by the store anytime you want. Bring your comics. They'll look at them and buy the ones they want."

"What'd you do?"

"I just talked to them business owner to business owner. Now let's get home, I'm tired."

"Me, too."

Some time passes quietly in the car.

"You know when that guy got me in the headlock? I really thought he was going to kill me. I was seeing stars."

"By the looks of your neck, he came close. I've given and received just as many headlocks as the next guy, but nothing like that. You say you know this kid?"

"Yeah, I know him."

"Next time, you get *him* in a headlock. Make him see stars for a little bit. He won't be so likely to be doing that to other people then."

"All right, Dad."

With Dad driving me home, in his Members Only jacket and with the smell of Old Spice, I almost feel normal again . . . almost.

After church on Sunday I swing by the Grab Bag Store and sell a few comic books and get thirty-five dollars in return before heading home, where I watch television all day while Dad works on that project of his in the backyard. He's taken those pipes back there and commenced sawing them to slightly different lengths. I notice the ends of the pipes are curved at the ends, kind of like those curvy straws you can get, but they're all curved at different angles. He keeps taking out an old folded piece of paper from his shirt pocket. I've never seen him so preoccupied, but he seems happy working on it. It was still difficult to believe he was making installation art. Maybe it's that fence he always told Mom he was going to build. I guess it really doesn't matter now.

CHAPTER 7

ANOTHER MONDAY MEANS ONE OF TWO THINGS: soy burgers or turkey wraps for lunch. All I can think about is food while I'm stuck in the faculty lounge having to borrow a copy of *Huckleberry Finn* from the teachers' personal library, which covers an entire wall next to the copying machine opposite the sofa and coffee table. I lost mine, and the school library is all checked out. In return for this favor I've agreed to lug a gym bag full of brand-new sneakers to the physical education office. The sneakers are the result of a donation program for needy children in the area that had been set up by Central of Sugweepo High School in the winter.

"Thanks for taking those shoes, Samuel," says Mrs. Bickerson. "Coach Calhoun really appreciates it. Isn't that right, Coach Calhoun?"

"Sure do," says Coach Calhoun, munching on a burger and flipping through a fitness magazine. He's wearing those tight gray short-shorts the coaches wear. And his bald head with its pigskin tone is extra shiny today. "Your service will be remembered," he says, without looking up.

I throw on my faded black backpack emblazoned with the school crest of a white camel and then the gym bag of sneakers. The damn thing is heavier than it looks. I have to lean forward and put my back into it. I exit the faculty lounge into the main hallway, where Tim Cutter walks toward me with the satisfied appearance of a guy who has just eaten lunch.

"What's for lunch?" I ask him as we pass each other.

"Burgers."

"Damn, I knew it," I say.

"They weren't that bad."

With my bag of sneakers in tow I bump into a like-minded crowd of hungry students heading toward the cafeteria, so I cut right and go up the north stairwell, where I cross over and go back down to the parallel hallway, which is always less busy. From there I leave the main building through the west exit and walk toward the gym.

The physical education office is locked. "Bastards," I say to myself. I'm stuck with a bag of sneakers and I can't stop thinking about a turkey wrap . . . actually what is on my mind is a gyro wrap. The only way I'm going to get a gyro wrap is to go off school grounds toting that thing. I go out to the front pickup curb, drop my bag, and call David on my cell phone.

There's no answer, so I try his other number, which is saved as "David Control." It's his work number, he told me. Joe walks by and says, "What up?" I nod back to him. David doesn't answer at all, so I pick up the bag to go it alone. Joe in the meantime stops and yells, "Hey, dude! Are those surfer shoes you're wearing?" with a smile of mockery. At first I think he's talking to me but I've never worn surfer shoes let alone know what they even look like. There's some chubby freckle-faced subfreshman up ahead of me. His face turns red and it looks like he's just going to keep walking, but he stops and turns.

"Yeah, they're surfing shoes," the subfreshman yells defiantly, and keeps going. His shoes look like beige-colored Chuck Taylors, except without the sole. *So that's what surfer shoes look like*, I think to myself.

"Who needs shoes to surf?" says David, coming toward me.

"I just tried to call you," I say.

"Did you call my work line?"

"Yeah."

"Shit." He pulls his phone out of his pocket. "What the hell's wrong with this thing?"

"Did you do it? Did you ask about Mrs. Greenan?" I ask.

"Yeah, I said I would, didn't I?"

"And you didn't mention my name, right?"

"Yeah, yeah. What about lunch? You had lunch yet?"

"I was going to the gyro place."

"Sounds good to me," he says. "What's with the sack?"

"I'll tell you on the way," and I do. David is one of the few students who cares less than me about going off campus. He and I are generally well liked among the teachers but for completely different reasons: I'm a straight-A student and help out the teachers with odd jobs; David supports his mother while somehow maintaining a B average, which probably means he's a genius, considering how much he skips class and doesn't study. As long as we don't make trouble and we're not caught leaving campus, we know we'll be okay. Being caught would just mean time in lockdown.

"So what'd you find out?" I ask.

"Mrs. Greenan went to Mobile for a couple of days."

"What about those babies?"

"I don't know—maybe she took them with her."

"That's impossible. I told you I heard them squawking from her house as I rode by on my bike."

"Since when do you care? Last time you were around those things you hurled all over her backyard."

"I just wasn't ready for it."

"Wasn't ready?"

"Yeah, wasn't ready. And now I just want to make sure they're okay."

"Whatever. Go ask her yourself."

"She hates me."

"No she doesn't. She told her sister, who told my mom, she felt bad for kicking you out . . ." We walk through the east student parking lot, weaving through the myriad of cars. I toss the gym bag over the wooden fence demarcating the end of campus and climb over. We then jump the ravine before crossing the green field that serves as a shortcut to the highway. We take our time under the late spring sun, knowing we'll probably be late for class and not caring one bit. The field rises slowly and then levels out onto Highway 67. We carefully cross over to the strip mall where the gyros await.

The first thing we do is stop by the Kroger store to get some cheap sodas. Then once in the gyro shop David and I get straight down to business. We each order two gyro wraps along with two large orders of fries. We eat methodically and slowly, with little conversation. Sometimes we laugh at ourselves with stuffed mouths, because of how silly we look and how happy we are eating. We eat until we're almost sick. David finishes everything while I leave a little bit of my second wrap.

"So how's the loan business going?" I ask him.

"Good. I'm prorating the loans. It hurts me in the short term, but it's good long term."

"I didn't think you were in it for long."

"If I'm lucky, this is gonna pay my college tuition. West Georgian, here I come." He takes a drink of Dr Pepper.

"Just be careful. Don't loan money to the wrong person."

"They're all the wrong people," he says. "Why else would anyone go to a tenth-grade high school student for a loan?"

"Other students are okay. I'm just saying be careful of grown-ups."

I sit for a moment looking around the restaurant and the sunny day outside. David looks at me and makes this crazy face. We have a good laugh.

"Have you taken your practice SAT yet?" he asks.

"I don't even want to think about that. Let's go, I still gotta drop these damn shoes off."

We walk back to school the way we came.

DAVID GOES INTO SCHOOL FROM the east entrance while I walk back around to the front. I'm already late for history, but I have to carry out my shoe delivery. Those are the orders from up on high. A couple basketball games are just beginning when I get to the gym. Coach Calhoun is in his office talking to some senior football players. He has a big fat ball of chewing tobacco in his right cheek, which he doesn't try to conceal from me or anyone else, for that matter.

"Where do you want 'em, Coach?" I ask.

"Over there." He nods to the corner, where two other gym bags already lay. I toss them down and head out. "Trying out for varsity this year?" he asks me.

"I don't think so, Coach. I'm just a benchwarmer on junior varsity. I'd be the same on varsity."

"Just making the team would be good enough for most."

I slowly turn the large globe that is sitting on his desk. My hand goes over Algeria and Libya. "Not for me."

"Think about it," he says. "Do it for your school, son."

"I'll think about it."

I walk out into the gym. On one of the side courts there is a game of two-on-three.

"Samuel! Come on! We need one more!" It's some guy from a grade ahead of me. Everyone is in there because it's an eleventh-grade P.E. class. I recognize most of their faces but not their names.

"I'm already ten minutes late for history," I say.

"Come on! One game! If you get to class late, it's not going to be the end of the world."

It seems like a good point, so I join in. The game begins, and I just hang back, passing and playing loose defense. The opposing team stays in control, but that isn't because they're any good. It's because we are so bad. My team looks like a bunch of uncoordinated cartoon characters running around and throwing the ball at the basket.

"You're getting spanked, man," says one of the guys after he makes a layup on us. It's a really big guy I know plays linebacker on the varsity football team. "It's not the end of the world for being late to history class. But it's going to feel like the end of the world after you lose this game."

I start making shots then. The best I could do on the junior varsity team was sit on the bench, but that was against tall athletic black guys who play basketball all the time. Compared to them, these guys are a walk in the park. I make six shots in a row and even start passing the ball away on the game-winning shot of fifteen to make it a fair game, but the other team keeps missing their shots, so I just end it with a baby hook.

"I forgive you for trying to end the world," I say to the big guy.

"What?" he asks.

"You said if my team lost it would feel like the end of the world, which meant you wanted to end the world because you wanted to win."

"Huh?" he says, and walks up to me with his chest out. I have the urge to punch him in the face even though he's a lot bigger than me. He'd probably kill me, so I just walk away.

I run to my history class hoping Mr. Garrett won't be too angry about my being late. The thing is, he's out in the hallway talking with Mr. Peck. I slow down to a fast walk.

"Samuel," says Mr. Garrett. "Mr. Peck here was just telling me about your little video project. He says it all came from a dream. Is that true?"

"Yes, sir," I say.

"So you're saying that's exactly how you saw it in your dream."

"Well, almost exactly."

"Oh, you left something out?" asks Mr. Peck. "What was it?"

"I forgot."

"Oh, one of those dreams?" Mr. Peck says.

"Yes, one of those dreams." I'm not sure I know what he means, so I add, "I'm going to be late for class now," and slip past them. I get to class and Mr. Garrett follows me in. Class goes like usual. I take my notes and try not to get too bored. When class is over, he tells us all that we will have an exam tomorrow. The old bastard must have had a bad day. He's usually laid back, so I don't get it. I even caught him picking his nose one time and didn't say anything. Now I'll have to study up. I plan on acing that exam.

WHEN CLASSES FINISH AT THREE, I take my history book to the school library and study at the tables beside the periodicals until it closes at five. Not only did I use my textbook but two others I found on the history shelves.

I walk over to the bike rack out front, where my blue Schwinn is locked up, and check my phone messages. Among others, there's one from Melody: "My daddy wants you to pick up that TV he fixed for you a month ago. You want to come and get it or what?" I call her right back. "Where you at?" she asks me.

"I'm still at school."

"Did you get into some kind of trouble?"

"I was studying for an exam. But I'm finished now."

"You want to come over and get your TV?" she asks. "If you don't, it's gonna get tossed."

"I can't. I rode my bike to school."

"You and your silly bike. You want me to pick your sorry butt up, don't you?"

"You don't have to . . ."

"Give me a few minutes."

I sit down on the curb and watch the occasional student walk by. There're still plenty of them about, what with baseball and track and chess and all the rest of it. There's a school activity for everyone these days, bug collectors to future problem solvers. What the hell would we do without them? Fifteen minutes later Melody pulls up in her dark blue Fiat. I leave my bike locked on the rack and get in. I like sitting in her car because it smells like incense. Melody looks at me and smiles through her coiled black hair. She smiles a long time, and it makes me want to jump out of the window.

"You shouldn't be so nice to people," I say.

"What?" She starts moving past the front pickup lane and out onto the main road.

"You're nice to everyone."

"What's wrong with that?"

"There're folks who might see that as a way to take advantage of you."

"Like who?"

"Those upperclassmen jock types I saw talking to you at lunch the other day."

"Ha. Jocks? You play basketball, so aren't you a jock?"

"I'm not going out this year," I say.

"Why not?"

"I just sit on the bench, anyhow."

"Get better then, dummy."

"I need to start getting ready for college. SATs and all that crap. Anyway, you shouldn't be so nice to those guys. They'll get the wrong idea."

"What? Are you jealous?"

"No, not at all. You just never know with guys like that. You can't trust them."

"Maybe if other guys were nice to me I wouldn't even talk to them," she says as we hit a stretch of bumpy road near the school that has been there forever. The wooden cross that hangs down from her rearview mirror taps against the windshield, and the awkward silence continues. There is a rubber band sitting on top of a pile of change in her ashtray. I take it and put it on my wrist where I pop it against my skin.

"Ouch," I say.

"What're you doin'?"

I pop my wrist again.

"Stop that." She tries to grab the rubber band from me.

"Here, you want it? You can have it." I place it on her wrist.

"You're out of your mind, boy," she says with a smile. She takes a deep breath and then becomes quiet again. It seems like she wants to say something more, but instead she grows very calm. We soon get to her house. "Listen, just wait in the car. I'll go in and get the TV."

"If your dad's home tell him thanks for fixing it pro bono and sorry it's taken me so long to pick it up. I've been distracted."

"Distracted, huh?" she says, and goes in. Her dad is using the home garage as a repair shop because the store where he worked laid him off. From what Melody tells me, he's doing okay on his own. She comes out with my old black-and-white television. She places it in my lap and walks around to the driver's side.

"Why don't you get a color TV? I'm sure my dad would just give you one if I asked. He's got like a dozen old ones he's fixed sitting around in the basement."

"I'll stick with the black-and-white."

We drive around on some country roads for a while just talking about school and life. It's easy to talk to her, especially driving around in her car like that.

"Something's different about you," she says to me.

"Like what?"

"I don't know. You don't seem the same. I mean, you look the same and even act the same, but there's something not right."

"Do you ever feel like there are terrible things in the world?"

"What terrible things?"

"That's what I mean. They're there but we don't see them. All we can do is go to school and horse around and pretend they're not there, out there, even inside us. It's all pretend . . . like everything is normal when it's not. It's all so fake and full of crap."

"What's wrong, Samuel?" She looks me right in the eyes, like she wants me to confess to her. That's what I feel, that she wants me to tell her everything. And I want to. I want to tell her about those babies and everything that's happened since, but shame wells up in my heart like an ugly face. I want to hide in the deepest hole I can find.

I can barely look at her let alone tell her anything. "Is this about your mom?" she asks pleadingly.

"My mom?" I start laughing. "Oh, no no. Nothing like that. It's . . . I've just been thinking too much. I'm okay now . . . adolescence you know," I said with a smile.

Melody laughs. "I wish you'd tell me what was going on up there," she says.

"It's empty," I say.

By the time she drops me off at home Dad's already there.

I GO INTO THE KITCHEN and find a dinner of steak and peas sitting on the table. Dad is out back working. I still can't really tell what exactly he's making as I watch through the window. He's taken the pipes and laid them on the ground along with a bunch of other stuff he's brought back from his hardware store. I eat dinner and have an ice-cream bar before hooking up the black-and-white television in my room. My mom had given it to me for a birthday present when I was ten. Jim had his own little TV and he wouldn't let me watch it sometimes, so Mom got that old black-and-white secondhand job just for me. We don't have cable so I have to attach the rabbit ears, and even with that I can only get about three and a half channels. I get a wire from the garage and attach one end to a rabbit ear and the other I toss out my window. I go out to get the other end.

"Did you eat?" Dad asks when he sees me out there.

"Yeah."

I get the ladder from the garage and go around to the other side of the house where my bedroom window is.

"Hey, you think you can help out this weekend at the store?" Dad hollers. "Tommy can't come in."

"Is it that busy?" I ask.

"If you've got plans, that's okay. I can make some calls."

"No, no, I'll come in."

I climb the roof, taking the wire with me, and attach it to the television antenna. The sky is a dark blue hue with an edge of crimson. A few stars are just beginning to flicker. It gets me to thinking about my mom for some reason. She's a ghost now, floating around up there somewhere. I stay on the roof awhile watching my dad tinkering with his pet project.

CHAPTER 8

THE NEXT MORNING I GET DAD TO DROP ME OFF at school on his way to work since my bike is still there. It gives me a chance to review my history textbook the whole way there.

"You gotta test?" Dad asks.

"Yeah, and I plan on acing the bastard."

Mom would have never let me say "bastard," but that's beside the point. I get back to flipping those pages. I'd always been a good student, but it wasn't until recently that I've felt compelled to ace everything. I didn't even know what college I wanted to go to. I didn't care. But if I had a test or exam to take, I did everything I could to get a good score. It wasn't even getting the good score that made me feel good. It was focusing on one thing and wiping everything else out of my head. That's when I felt best. That's when I felt nothing.

Dad drops me off, and I go through algebra and then Spanish

class with history on my mind. It isn't until Mr. Peck's art class that I forget about that test. I really enjoy art class. Mr. Peck allows us students to do whatever we want as long as we produce. Robert, an upperclassman with premature white hair, had originally approached me about doing a documentary about the basketball team before I made my own video. Later on he dumped me as a partner to do something on his own. Actually his hair is more gray than white, and he keeps it pointing straight up somehow. Everybody thinks he's cool and talented, but I think it's more his hair than anything else.

At the beginning of class that day Robert gets everyone to stop what they're doing and come into the small auditorium to watch a short video sketch he made. Once everyone in the class comes in and sits down, Robert announces that he was inspired by Andy Warhol and is going to make a full-length film based on this sketch. He turns on the television in front of the small stage and squats down to turn on the video player. The video shows him and another fellow with white hair going into some abandoned theater. Where did he find another guy with prematurely graying hair? The two white-haired guys walk through that abandoned theater up onto the stage, where they start talking about waterfalls. Then it cuts to them at an actual waterfall somewhere in the woods. Robert's standing by it then the other guy appears riding a blue canoe. He takes the canoe over the waterfall and disappears into the foam at the base of the falling water, then pops back up and continues canoeing down the river. I don't catch the rest of the film because I keep looking out a window into the gym, which is connected to the auditorium. On the main court I can see a big fat kid dominating the area around the basket. He's pushing people around down there, and no one is calling a foul. The other team keeps coming at him though, double-teaming him on defense and attacking him on offense. When I turn back to the video I see Melody, watching me from down the row. I bend down and pretend to tie my shoelace. When I sit back up the short video sketch ends, and Mr. Peck comes in.

"This isn't Robert's appreciation time. Get back to work. That includes you three," he says to three Asian girls sitting on the small stage at the back of the auditorium. Everyone starts slowly moving back into the art room.

Robert and Tim, this other artsy hipster, start talking to Melody. Robert sees me and walks over with a nod of his head.

"So what did you think?" he asks me.

"You should run with it. I'll work on something on my own. This is something you have to go with," but I'm thinking, *You jackass*.

"Thanks. I was worried you would be lost without me. What do you think about Melody?"

"She's okay," I say.

"You know, maybe you could be next in line for a try at her."

I have the urge to hit him on the head with a chair. "I'll have to remember that," I say, and walk away. I ditch the rest of art class and play basketball. Mr. Peck is back in his office and won't even notice. He probably wouldn't have said anything anyway. I jog to the locker room and change into shorts and a T-shirt and then go back into the gym, where I find a game. By the time I finish playing, third period has already ended. It's time to go to homeroom, which means lunch. My real P.E. class is right after lunch. There's no point in showering and changing when I'm going to get sweaty again, so I stay in my shorts and T-shirt. I walk to my homeroom, which is Mrs. Bickerson's class on the south end of the building. Mrs. Bickerson is okay, other than the fact that she's got these wispy white hairs on her chin that look kind of like a beard. She doesn't even notice me coming in late. Or maybe she just doesn't care any longer. Everyone else is there already at their desks, wiling away the time. I get a seat against the wall beside Will and take my shoes and socks off before stretching out my legs. My hair is still wet with sweat, and the endorphins are still pumping through my brain.

"Where you been?" Will asks me, taking a drink from a bottle of Gatorade. I've noticed these days he smells like marijuana most of the time. Ever since he started playing bass in a local country punk band with some guys from the Sugweepo High swim team, he smells like ganja. I've gone to a couple of their practices in their basement, and smoking weed preceded the playing both times. I figured it was the source of his musical inspiration. We don't hang out as much since he's turned into a semi-pro rock star, but it's probably for the better. His pranks annoy the hell out of me.

"Art class," I say.

"Must be some heavy art," he says.

"I ditched and shot some hoop. Did Bickerson call roll?" I ask.

"Yeah."

I raise my hand. "Mrs. Bickerson! I'm here!" I yell.

"I saw you," she says, without looking up.

I lean my head back against the white wall, and for a moment it feels like I'm not in school. I'm on a tropical beach and have just toweled myself off after having a swim in the cool waters of the sea. Then a shark lunges out of the water, and the lunch bell rings. I jump up front along with Will and Brad in my bare feet. They both seem as hungry as me as we three jog up the hallway ahead of everyone else. Today is the day Mrs. Bickerson's homeroom gets to be first to lunch. As we make it onto the floor, Will thinks it would be funny to toss some of the water in his bottle onto the floor.

"What're you doing that for?" I ask. He just smiles and walks into the serving room. My bare feet feel nasty on the cold wet floor. "Bastard," I say. I know I'll be giving up my place in line, but I jog past my homeroom whose just getting to the cafeteria.

"Where you goin'?" someone asks.

"My shoes," I say.

I jog back to our classroom, but the door is locked. Other classes are already starting toward the cafeteria, so I hurry back, taking the shortcut through the darkly lit game room, which connects the main hallway with the cafeteria. Some kid is actually in there playing one of those four ancient video-game machines. My homeroom is already seated and eating. The rest of the tenth-grade class is lined up. These other guys won't let me cut, not when I'm not in their homeroom. I'll have to go to the end of the line, which is all the way down the hall.

I walk over to the serving room and see that they're serving sweet-and-sour chicken. I think, *To hell with it, I'll just get in the other line, which is much shorter.* There're two serving rooms in the cafeteria. The lesser of the two meals is served in the second line. If it's meat loaf in the first line, it's usually Spam in the other, or if it's hamburgers in the first line, it's ham sandwiches in the second. I usually avoid the second line, as do most other students, but there's no way in hell I'm waiting in that first line.

So I get in the second, much shorter line, and what do you know? It's the same food. I get up to the counter, and the server, a young black guy who doesn't look too much older than me, gives me a plate of brown fried rice. I forgo the usual chocolate milk and get a cola. A short curly-haired girl I've seen around, who's standing behind me, smiles and puts a straw in my Coke for me. I smile back at her and her big boobs. Then she puts in a few more straws and giggles before walking away with her girlfriend. My glass has about ten straws in it. The server is staring at my drink, too.

"Hey, what about the chicken?" I ask.

"They ain't no meat left here. Go over there," he says.

He points toward the end of the cafeteria, where the old soda machines sit dormant on an unused table. I walk toward the ice machine and see a buffet with two trays of chicken and what looks to be pepperoni or some sort of thinly sliced red meat. Brad is getting some meat, too.

"Man, there's not much left, and this is my first time around," I say.

"I'm just getting a little extra meat for my sandwich," he says before sitting down. That's right. Brad always brings his lunch from home. Everybody knows that.

I get some chicken and sit down in front of Brad. I can't help noticing Katy and her girlfriends sitting at the next table. The rumor around our grade is that I like her. But it's not true. She's cute, but I'm just not that interested. I act as nonchalant as I can around her, hoping to kill the rumor, but you can't kill a rumor. It has to die out on its own or be replaced. Brad suddenly pulls this nacho out of his brown bag and starts talking about it. "Look how brittle and dry it is," he says. "Look at it." He holds it up to the sunlight coming in through the large cafeteria windows. The light reflects off of its yellow body, making it look almost diaphanous. "It's gotten dry and stale. It's dangerous. This thing is so brittle, so old that, if I stabbed myself in the ankle it would break my skin and bleed . . ."

He keeps going on and on. It's impressive how much he can talk about that nacho. I'm too busy stuffing my mouth with rice and sweet-and-sour chicken to respond to his nacho soliloquy.

". . . something needs to be done about this nacho . . ." he continues.

Then with a mouthful of food, I say offhandedly, "You exaggerate." After a slight pause I start laughing with all this rice and chicken in my mouth. I can't control myself. Brad's face turns red, and he has his eyes closed he's laughing so hard. This Christian girl from my class is sitting alone a couple of seats down from Brad. She's one of these serious hard-core Christian girls who I have never seen talking to anyone except her twin sister. She must have overheard us because her face is redder than Brad's. This goes on for quite some time, and we three can't seem to control ourselves. Other kids are staring and asking what's so damn funny, but I really don't know either. Tears are coming down my cheeks I'm laughing so hard.

"I'm sorry," I say, trying to catch my breath. "It's my fault." Slowly the laughing subsides and we get back to eating. Across from us Katy and her friends are watching a video iPod. They're trying to guess the name of some classic sitcom that's on. I lean over to take a look.

"Oh, it's *The Jeffersons*!" Brad says immediately before I can even answer.

Debbie says, "Brad's got it right. He's one ahead of you, Samuel."

I look at Brad and say, "I should be up a ton on you just because of what I said just a second ago."

"Don't say anything, Samuel," he says, holding his stomach. And for a minute, having that laugh at lunchtime on a sunny afternoon, I remember what it feels like to be a normal high school kid. And I wish it could always be like that.

CHAPTER 9

I GET HOME AND PUT MY BIKE AWAY before hopping in my car. Sitting there behind the wheel, thinking to myself, the memory of the day at school seems so absurd when I weigh it against that night at Mrs. Greenan's, about the babies and that greasy bastard, my own feelings . . . it's this double life, and one end is a whole lot heavier than the other. But I don't know any other way to live. I don't know what to do. Why do I even think about going back there? To help the lady and the babies? I don't care about her, and I want those things to disappear. But at the same time I want to know . . . I need to know what's happening to them. I start the car, and within twenty minutes I'm parking in front of the house. Dusty and his brother are out in their front yard playing around with mud when I pull up to Mrs. Greenan's house. The lawn has been mown and the hedges around the house neatly trimmed since the last time.

"Hey! You came back!" yells Dusty.

"No thanks to you, Judas," I say.

"It all happened too fast. I didn't have time."

"Forget about it," I say, and start going in.

"Where're you going?" he asks. He just stays put as I go up to the porch. I can hear his big brother calling him back to their front yard, back home. Before I knock I can see a figure behind the screen door and my hackles rise and my adrenaline revs up. But it's only Mrs. Greenan. "Samuel, come on in." She leads me through the foyer into the living room. The house is well lit, all the drapes are open, letting in light, and everything's tidy like the very first time I came to visit. There're even some fresh flowers in a vase on the coffee table.

"I just wanted to apologize again for the way I acted that day," I say.

"It's okay, Samuel. When Margaret told me about your momma dying at such an early age, I thought, That poor boy. And you came back to apologize. Nobody's ever done that. I felt bad the moment you left. How about some sweet tea?"

"No thanks, ma'am. I just wanted to see how those babies were doing. Is there any way I could take a peek?"

"Sure, you could. They're taking a nap upstairs, so be quiet."

"Don't worry, I know how to be quiet."

I follow her up those stairs, and I put my hand on the cold smooth banisters. We get to the room, the same room where I almost became a murderer and was almost murdered at the same time. But just like the living room, it's clean and tidy now. The hardwood floor has been picked up and the stench had been replaced with pine. The three babies are huddled together, eyes closed and breathing steadily on the well-made bed. They almost look normal like that, sleeping together. Almost human. Was the other night even real? How could this be? I nod my head to Mrs. Greenan, and we walk back down.

"Sure you don't want some tea or cookies? They're homemade."

"Actually I just wanted to see them one time," I say.

Then from the kitchen a cold voice says, "We got a guest in the house?"

"Sure do, Daryl. It's Samuel. Samuel Polk, that boy I told you about."

It's those heavy boots walking out of the kitchen. He's wearing the greasy-looking blue baseball cap over that longish dark hair. I get a good look at that cap for the first time. It's one of those old Braves baseball caps from back in the seventies and eighties, with the 'a' in little letters, worn by the likes of Dale Murphy and Hank Aaron. I don't know whether I should run, warn Mrs. Greenan, or call the cops.

"I was really sorry to hear about your mother," he says with a toothpick hanging out the side of his mouth. He holds out his hand. "It must have been such a shock at such an early age." I look at his hand and see the old cut wounds on his forearm. "Don't mind that, that's from huntin' skunk." He smiles a big yellow-toothed smile.

I see Mrs. Greenan looking at me and then at my hand. So I take his hand and shake it. He squeezes it real hard with that smile on his face. I have to hold down a scream, his grip is so damn hard. Then he lets go with a friendly nod. "Sure you don't want some cookies?" he asks. "They're homemade."

"Who are you?" My voice breaks as I ask.

"Daryl? Daryl's my son," she says with a laugh. "He helps me with my little miracles."

"Yup. What with looking after those little miracles, working at the sewage plant, huntin', and singin' in my rock band, I barely even got time to eat."

"I just wanted to see your little ones to make sure they were all right. That's all."

"Why wouldn't they be all right?" asks Daryl.

"Had a bad dream, that's all."

"Bad dream? Don't be stupid," says Daryl. "Ha-ha-ha! He came over here because of a bad dream. He's a strange one, isn't he?"

"He sure is," said Mrs. Greenan. "You sure have a lot of bad dreams." She turns to Daryl. "Why, I found him having one on our steps not long ago."

"Really? Why didn't you tell me?" With fists clenched, he steps up to Mrs. Greenan, who takes a step back.

"I did! I did!" she pleads. "Just the other day."

"That's right, you did," he says.

"I'll be going now," I say, and head for the front door as fast as I can.

"You come back now when you're ready for some tea and cookies."

"How many times you gonna ask him about those goddamn cookies? Can't you see he don't want any?"

I'm already out of there: down the porch, across the front yard. I'm walking fast. The screen door slams, and I turn around. Daryl comes running down.

"Stop!" I yell with my hands out.

"I knew you'd come." He puts his arm around my shoulder. "Don't worry, Samuel Polk, I didn't tell nobody."

"Tell what?"

"Come on, don't bullshit me. You're a natural-born murderer."

"No way. You were forcing me," I say.

"I didn't make you do nothin'. You did it on your own. Now get in the fucking car." He opens his car door and pushes me in. "I know you ain't gonna lie about not doing it because, Samuel, you couldn't live with a lie like that." *God, this guy terrifies me.* I get the feeling he could do something insane and terrible at any moment.

Why me? And how the hell could he be the son of Mrs. Greenan? She's so nice.

He starts the Charger and speeds out of the neighborhood, squealing his tires. I should have never let him get me in the car. *Think, stupid.* But it's too late. "Don't be a faggot, Samuel Polk! Man up! You are what you are."

"Did you hit your mom?"

He punches me in the arm with a fist that feels like a baseball bat. "That dummy. She's a terrible mom. Not smart enough. Sometimes I wonder how I was born out of that thing. Look what done come out of her. Either them babies or me is wrong for this world. It's either me or them, Samuel. It sure as hell ain't me," he says, and pulls over onto the side of the road. "Here," he says. "Put this over ya." He takes out the stinking burlap bag.

"Why?"

"It's for your own protection," he says, bringing his hunting knife from the back of his pants. I take the bag and pull it over my head all the way down to my arms and chest. In the darkened amber haze I can feel the car get back on the road.

"You drove by that day when I was studying on the porch steps," I say.

"Yup. And I saw you at the fair, too. You're crazy, you know that? Climbing up that thing like that. Remember this?" He screams, "'Go, you fucking monkey!' That was me. And then falling back like that, whew. I knew you were insane then. I knew you were capable of anything."

"So you were following me?"

"Who's following who, you stupid shit?" He pushes my head down hard to my knees. "Duck your head down." I hear more traffic for a while, which means we were going into town. He pulls into somewhere and then drives around some and finally stops. It's quiet here and there's a new bad smell, like garbage coming in through the stench of the bag. Then he jerks me out of the driver's side with him and starts leading me toward some unknown destination. I'm walking on hard earth and grass and bushes and brambles, and I can hear birds calling and the faint rustle of branches. I can see shadows and faint light through the crosshatch of the bag.

"How much longer?" I say. He doesn't answer and pushes me on. Time passes and we're walking and I'm sweating bullets under that bag. Then I hear animals scurrying about, getting louder and louder until they're up close. A door creaks open, and I'm pushed inside a room with a wooden floor. He finally pulls the bag from over me, bringing in a fresh batch of cool air. I'm in a dirty little shed about the size of my bedroom, furnished with a small military cot and a worktable covered with dried blood and tools. The walls are covered with little skulls and animal hides: squirrel, opossum, cat, dog, skunk, and more, but I can't tell all of them. There's the one door and a few smudged windows, through which I see woods.

"It's my huntin' shed," he says, and slams the knife down in the table, making it stick straight up. "Sit down." I sit down on the cot, and he goes out. I look for a way out, maybe I can make a bum's rush for the door or knife, but he's already coming right back in holding a wooden pine box the size of a small television. He places the box in front of me. A raccoon's head struggles to free itself at the top of the box, where there's a hole cut in it. The box is composed of two parts that are locked together at the base of the hole, trapping the head. Daryl hands me a hammer. "This is practice for a runt like you."

"I don't understand . . ."

"Ha. You'll kill a kid but not a raccoon?"

"I didn't kill anyone."

"Because I stopped you, you murderer." He pulls up his britches by the legs and bends his knees like he's in the middle of a huddle.

"Now watch how it's done." He cocks the hammer back, and as he brings it down I look away.

"Ahhhh!" I yell, but it can't cover the whacking sound the hammer makes on the raccoon's head.

"It screams just like a baby!" he says. "Look at it!"

"Hell no!"

I feel the hammer come down on my back. "Ahhh!" I raise my arms to protect myself. He kicks me a few times and goes back to finishing off the raccoon, which has stopped screaming.

"It's over, faggot! You can look now."

I keep my head turned with my hands over my face.

"Look, goddamnit." He grabs me and turns me around, jerking my hands away. There's just the bloody hole at the top of the box. "See, if you do it right, and you beat the head to a pulp, it just slips through the hole and it's already in its casket. I made a bigger one for when we do those demon freaks. But the same thing. Wait." He slips out of the door and I make a break for it, but he's right there waiting for me. He punches me right in the solar plexus and pushes me down. "I said, Wait."

I lie on the ground for a while trying to catch my breath. Outside I can hear him manhandling another animal. How can this be happening? I wonder while looking at the blood staining the wooden floors and walls. Then he comes back in with the box and a cat head meowing and squirming about at the top.

"Here, get up." He grabs me by the shoulders and pulls me up, sitting me on the cot. "Now do like I did. Spread your legs and bend your knees. The power comes from your legs." He slaps his thighs. "Got it?" He puts the hammer in my hands, which I let drop to the floor. He walks over to the table and gets the knife. Then he starts cutting himself on the arms like last time.

"Good!" I say. "More. Cut more. You sick bastard!" He grabs

my arm, pulls back the sleeve, and makes a cut in my arm. "Ahh, stop!"

"Hit it! Just like you would if it were one of those little monsters."

"Why? It didn't do anything to anyone."

"No one does anything to anyone. Doesn't mean they can't die. There's no God. We're all flesh and blood." He slaps both his arms. "That's all there is, then we die! Just like your mother."

I shake my head.

"No? If there was a God, you think he'd let your momma die like that? While you're still a boy who needs his momma? You think he'd put her and you through that kind of pain? Can't you see? It's all nothing. We can do what we want. It don't mean nothing! We're free! Now hit."

"Wait! Give me a minute." He cuts my arm again. "Ahhhh, shit! Okay, okay! I'll do it!" I'm crying now, staring at him. I want to kill him, but he's got the knife.

"What are you waiting for? Do it."

"You do it!"

"Hell, you already got blood on your hands. You've got a destiny to follow."

"What?"

"You killed your momma."

"Who told you that?" I say. Using his free hand he pinches the crap out of my side. "Ahhh!"

"You murdered her," he says. "It was your fault."

"Shut up." He puts the blade up to my neck. "You want me to do it?" I say.

"No shit, Sherlock fucking Holmes! C'mon, killer!"

"Okay, watch this, you son of a bitch!"

I take the hammer and turn away from him so I'm between him

and the box. I start hitting as hard as I can just below the cat's head, where the lock connecting the two pieces of the box is. I strike again and again. Sparks fly, and wood begins to splinter at the metal hinges. I want to destroy it all.

"Yeah! That's more like it!" he says over my shoulder. "Aim better, idgit! You're too damn low!"

The entire front of the box collapses, and the box splits open and out from where it connected on the hinges in the back. The cat scampers out.

"You goddamn idgit!" Daryl gets low, trying to catch the cat, and when he does I smack him straight on top of his head with the hammer. It sounds like a thud. "Ohhh!" He brings his hands to his head. Then I hammer on the hand holding the knife. "Goddamn!" he screams. The knife clatters to the floor. I grab it and start backing to the door. "You little bastard! Do you know who I am?" he screams, holding his wrist. In response, I throw the hammer at his face then run out through the door. Outside there's a clearing in the middle of the woods bordered by a chain-link fence coming down one side. I start running through the clearing of dirt and weeds and see a light trail through the woods. My hooded walk here seemed almost straight on, so it would make sense that it would be there. I take one look back as Daryl comes staggering out of the door. The shed looks homemade, with a slanted tin roof and gray rotted wood built against the side of a dirt ridge. Beside the shed are a few cages, some empty and some containing an assortment of small animals, another raccoon and a rabbit . . . I don't look long. Daryl's coming. I start down the path as fast as I can run, not looking back even once. Running full speed, I get to the end of the path in what seems like a few minutes. *God, I hope that cat got away, too*. At the end of the trail I find Daryl's car parked beside three industrial-size trash bins. It's the small parking lot behind the Kmart. I walk quickly past the big grated doors where the distribution trucks back in to make their deliveries. I slip the knife in the back of my pants. It's cold on my lower back and ass. I take off my shoes and then my socks, which I use to wipe the blood and then tie around the cuts on my forearm. Luckily the socks are blue, which makes it hard to spot the blood. They just look darker. After I put my shoes back on I run around to the front. The traveling fair is long gone, and the dull Kmart parking lot looks the lonelier for it. The afternoon shoppers are out, some with kids, some pushing red shopping carts coming in and out of those automatic glass doors that go *whoosh* when I go in. I walk down the air-conditioned aisles of neatly shelved products to the back, where I find a water fountain and bathroom. I call Melody and tell her my car's in the garage and I got a ride out to Kmart, where I'm now stranded. I try to sound normal, but it's real hard. It's like I'm standing outside of my body watching myself talk. I feel like I'm stammering and stuttering, but she seems to understand all right.

"Give me fifteen minutes," she says.

"Remember . . . park at the front doors," I say.

I clean my cuts in the bathroom and rewrap the socks around real tight. I stay in the back until it's time and then go wait just inside the doors, keeping a sharp lookout for Daryl and his white Charger. When Melody pulls up, I run to her car, pulling out the knife before I sit down so as to not cut off a butt cheek.

"Jesus, what is that about?" she yells.

"Ah, I just bought it."

"You just bought it? Just like that. No bag or anything, just in your pants."

"Yeah, let's go."

She drives out of the parking lot with an eye on the knife. "What's up with those socks on your arm? Is that blood? Oh my God!"

"Calm down! It was an accident. I didn't know how sharp it was."

"Let me see."

"It's no big deal."

"Do we need to go to the hospital?"

"No! No hospital. I'm telling you, I'm fine . . . now . . ."

"What do you need a knife like that for, anyway? That's like the biggest knife I've ever seen."

"Could you just get me home?"

"Okay, okay."

She takes us on the bypass, cutting through the edge of town toward my house. I'm too busy trying to blot out what just happened to pay attention to Melody. But I stop my racing mind and say, "Thanks for picking me up like this."

"What's going on, Samuel?"

"It's nothing."

"If you don't want to tell me, it's okay. But I want you to know, you can tell me anything, Samuel, whether it's about school or family, anything."

"School's fine."

"What about your family? Your dad? Jim?"

"What about them?"

"I don't know, Samuel. I'm just saying maybe it can be hard at times with your mom gone."

"My mom? It's been a year, Melody. One fucking year. We've all got to move on, and I have. Maybe you should, too."

She doesn't even pull into my driveway, just stops in the road in front of my house.

"I'm sorry, Samuel. I won't bring up your mother again."

"I'm sorry. There's other stuff going on. I shouldn't have said what I did. Don't get too angry with me."

"I'm not angry."

"You look angry."

She takes a deep breath; her long lashes close and her face changes. The stern face turns into a smile, a smile so loving and disappointed I prefer the frown. "Out," she says. I get out and watch her drive away. I deserved her anger; that's what I think. But there's nothing she can do for me. She wouldn't understand. Hell, even I don't. It's too damn dark. Too evil. After she's gone I get my bike and go back out to Underwood as fast as I can. Thank God the Charger isn't there. I throw my bike in my Tempo and get the hell out of there.

FIRST THING I DO IS slip the knife under my mattress. Then, after a hot shower, I clean up my cuts with rubbing alcohol and Band-Aids. I make sure to put on a long-sleeve shirt before holing up in my room watching my black-and-white television all Friday night and Saturday. Among all the boob-tube fodder I catch a few episodes of *The Three Stooges* during a rain delay for a baseball game. I can't believe I never noticed how violent it is. Those three guys beat the crap out of each other. Especially Moe. The eye gouging, head bonking, hair pulling he does to Larry and Curly is ridiculous. When my dad comes in, I pretend to be studying. Saturday night rolls around, and it feels like a normal state of life is getting harder and harder to get back to, and I start to wondering, How much would it take to be lost from it all forever? To shake that awful mood, I go up on the roof to look at the stars and at my dad tinkering on his project some more. He's digging a small trench out to a spot in the yard where there's a shallow hole in the ground the width of a car tire. I'm thinking some kind of fountain, but I'm still not really sure. All I know is watching him slowly working and occasionally rubbing his chin in thought makes me feel a little better.

CHAPTER 10

I GET UP EXTRA EARLY ON TUESDAY because it's the morning when students apply for their lockers, parking spaces, and new identification cards for the next year. It's first come, first serve, starting with the juniors on down to the subfreshmen. The juniors had their chance the previous week. Now it's the sophomores' turn for the next two mornings.

Dad's gone by the time I head out. It's still about an hour before school starts, but I know there'll be a hell of a line to deal with, so I skip the usual cereal and plan on picking up some fast food along the way. The problem starts when my car makes this horrible grinding sound on the road. Telling Melody my car was broken probably jinxed me. I think about turning around, but I'm not too far from the place I know Dad goes to in the morning for breakfast. I decide to try him there. I turn onto Highway 166 and take exit 12, where Roscoe's Café is. I can see Dad's big tan Monte Carlo in the parking lot, and then as I pull in I see him standing there talking with this other guy. That grinding sound from my car gets their attention. The friend waves to my dad and goes to his car.

"When did that start?" Dad asks me after I park.

"Halfway here. I would've gone back home, but I thought I might catch you."

"Here, take my car today." He gives me his keys. "I'll stop by Bill's garage. He can give me a ride to work. Come by the store at five. Okay?"

"Okay." I get out, and Dad gets in. "Where'd you get that paper?" I ask him.

"Here, take it. I'm finished anyway. You might want to try the sausage biscuit here."

I go in the café and have a look around. Everyone in there's black except me. I get a sausage biscuit and coffee before heading off to school in Dad's car. His Monte Carlo's so wide, compared to my Tempo, I have trouble maneuvering. It's like driving a boat and the pickup is weak, but once it gets moving, it's smooth and heavy. I eat my biscuit along the way. Parking in the school parking lot is a pain, too. I never realized the parking spaces were so narrow. Fortunately, it's still early, so there aren't any cars around my space. I have to back out and repark three times to get the spacing right. I hurry to the office.

The line isn't as bad as I thought it would be. In fact, I'm shocked at how short it is. But then I hear, "No breaking, Samuel," coming from behind me.

"Breaking? Where's the end of the line?" I ask.

The line actually goes out of the office and spills into the hall, all the way down as far as the eye can see. I start walking toward the end of the line then find myself in front of David.

"How long you been waiting?" I ask.

"Too long. You think you're gonna break in line?"

"Maybe. Why don't they just make it in alphabetical order?" I ask.

"What are you talking about? I'd still be in the middle. Mabry with an 'M.'"

"Ah, that's right. But at least you'd know where to go."

"You smell like a sausage biscuit from Roscoe's," says Carlita, a tall, pretty black girl who giggles a lot. She's standing in front of David.

"A sausage biscuit and coffee," I say, holding up my coffee cup with my newspaper in my armpit. She giggles. Then I realize I might actually get away with breaking in line. It makes me feel like I'm the older guy fooling a bunch of kids. It's strange, like I'm out of place, like I should be somewhere else, maybe college or maybe at some job. I feel composed and resentful toward all these high school students for bringing me down to their level. They seem stupid and for a minute I hate them. I hate them so much I wish they were gone. This hatred I feel makes me sick to my stomach. Worst of all, I know it's not really them but me. Standing in that hallway with all those kids in line, I start getting that cold murky feeling. It's all in my mind. It has to be, because those fluorescent lights are still shining in the hallway, and there's no reason to feel this way. But I get this image in my head of greasy Daryl with his blue cap running down the hall with that knife in his hand, all in this bluish gloomy light. I know it's just my imagination, but my heart starts racing.

"Give me some of your coffee, Samuel," says Carlita, breaking my inner panic.

"You can have the rest," I say. I give her my cup, and she resumes her conversation with some of her girl buddies. "Listen, let's do this together," I say to David. "We can do it faster."

In the office there's a machine we have to put our previous school identification card in. From that card the machine spits out two more pictures on a piece of glossy paper. Using a little customized ruler, you have to cut it out with a paper cutter. The two pictures are placed on two different forms: one goes to the school, and the other one is supposed to be placed in your locker with the lock after cleaning it out on the last day of school. I tell David we can split the duties and get it done faster. I'll do the pictures and the cutting, and he can do the forms. He agrees, and my breaking in line becomes official.

When our turn comes, we go into the office. I ask David to give me the measurements off the pictures. He says sixty by twenty. I start measuring, but the problem is my hand starts shaking. I try to steady it with my right hand, but it doesn't help, so I put them both in my pocket.

"What's wrong with you?" he asks.

"Too much coffee," I say. "I got shaky hands. David, you do this."

We switch roles: I fill out the forms while David measures and cuts. He tells me his birth date and other essentials, which I write down with a shaky old man's hand on his form. It takes only about five minutes and we're both out of there.

Thanks to breaking in line I get to chemistry class early. A few other kids have gotten there before me. I see Melody sitting in the back, and just seeing her makes me feel a little better and my hands feel steady. Instead of sitting up front like I usually do, I sit down beside Melody, who's busy studying. She looks at me like I'm crazy. I'm sure she's wondering why I'm sitting beside her like this. I can't remember the last time we interacted at school. I don't care. Sitting by her makes me feel better. Normal. Like the shades being lifted at Mrs. Greenan's house. It makes all the difference in the world.

"Are you okay?"

"Yeah. Now I am. Did you get a good spot?" I ask, like everything in the world is hunky-dory.

"Yeah, I got a space in the east parking pot."

"Nice."

"What are you doing?"

"I got one in the west lot, but it's pretty close. You're studying the periodic table again, huh?"

"I mean, what are you doing, sitting beside me talking? You never do that."

From the back office Mrs. Lane yells, "Melody, remember to study!" in a very sarcastic voice.

"Wow, she's psychic," I say.

"Shouldn't she be encouraging me to study?"

"You're fine. What'd you get on that last quiz?"

"Ninety."

"See. I haven't even cracked my book. Just study the notes and handouts she gives you. All the quiz materials come from that. If you do it that way, you hardly have to even study." While I'm speaking a little voice comes into my head, saying, *Shit! Why the hell are you so confident?* But I keep talking.

"Are you sure?" she says.

"Yes, I'm sure. Remember what I got on that quiz?"

"Yeah."

"Didn't even open my book."

She takes out her notes and examines them. I take out my summer reading list, which Mrs. Bickerson gave us the previous week. The last book on the list had shocked the crap out of me. It's a poet by the name of Florence Cain, who I've read before in one of Jim's college literature books. Her poems are very short but for some reason I really like them and I don't even like poetry. But her poems make me think that such things can't possibly be made up by the human mind. I vaguely remember some lines that go something like:

The sun ebbed on the blood,
Buoyancy,
Fluency, gottlob,
Try to leave on the noon.

At least that's the way I remember it. Chemistry class soon begins. I really don't like chemistry that much because it includes two extra hours of lab twice a week. But the good thing about the class is that I find it rather easy. Another thing that makes chemistry okay is our teacher, Mrs. Lane. She's kind of obese, almost two hundred pounds, but it isn't because she eats a lot. She has glandular problems and whenever she wears short-sleeve shirts I can see all these moles on her arms. Something isn't right about her physically, but she's really nice, and all the students get along with her. A lot of it has to do with her age. She's young, in her mid-twenties, so she can relate to us better than the older teachers. At the end of the day's class, Mrs. Lane even takes us outside and shows us her new Mazda Miata. It seems funny that such a large lady would get such a small car, but she's sure happy about it. There's a fancy bike rack attached to the back bumper. It turns out she did marathon biking. I can't imagine her riding a bike, but if her obesity is glandular, maybe she's healthier than she looks. I get the feeling there's a lot I don't know about her. As class ends, Melody asks me one more time if I want to talk about something. I tell her no.

AFTER BIOLOGY I GO TO homeroom. We're last on the list for lunch that day, so we'll have to wait. Mrs. Bickerson must have been in a good mood because she takes the entire class outside to the soccer field. The soccer field is this big depression in the ground on the other side of the school from the football field. Concrete bleachers are carved into the embankment of the depression on the side of the field closest to the school. The other side is just a shallow ditch that runs into the woods. Mrs. Bickerson takes attendance, and then we just hang out for twenty minutes on the bleachers. It's a little hot, but there's a nice breeze. I ask Katy, who's sitting up a bleacher from me, what's for lunch. She says, "Ahhhh . . ." And then asks Debbie.

"You don't need to do that," I say.

"Sloppy joes," Debbie says.

When it's finally time for lunch and we all go to get in line, I notice some gum stuck on my pants. Luckily it's really old gum, so it's already kind of hardened. I wipe it off with some paper without making a mess of it. I have to run up to get a decent space in line and then get squeezed out as kids from the back push forward. Those of us who get squeezed out call out our spot so we don't lose our place.

"I'm behind Debbie!"

"I'm behind Branden!"

I yell, "I'm behind Katy!" and try to squeeze back in. I joke, "Wow, if this were the end of the world we'd really get the squeeze!"

Katy laughs and says, "Yeah. And you could run away and later tell them how they're not invited to your barbecue."

The barbecue is a running joke made up by Will, who one day told everyone I was having a barbecue. If I hadn't heard about it, there would have been a ton of people showing up at my house on that Sunday afternoon. I had to announce to everyone in our grade that there was no barbecue. Even still to that day occasionally someone asks me how the barbecue went. Mrs. Bickerson is leading us into the cafeteria the back way, through the kitchen. We go through this large storage area, where high shelves are stocked with boxes and gigantic cans of creamed corn and beans. The janitor and a couple of the coaches are having lunch in there on a foldout table. It looks like a good place to eat lunch.

"Coming in from the back door?" asks Coach Simpson.

"You got to try something different sometimes," Mrs. Bickerson says. It sounds almost as if she were joking a little. I've never heard her even try to joke. Mrs. Bickerson tells us to hurry up and that lunchtime is practically almost over. "No dillydallying," is how she puts it. The cafeteria is packed, so I go ahead and get the first empty seat I can find beside Will. I put my backpack on the table before getting back in line behind Katy. I'm served a plate of sloppy joes, fries, and beans and sit down. Will grins at me, his mouth full of food, and the only thing I see for a split second are Daryl's nasty yellow-brown teeth. I suddenly have this ridiculous urge to brush my own teeth. I turn Will's head with my hand. "Not today, man." I try to go ahead and eat but it's too much, so I run to the restroom and rinse my mouth out with water. When I get back to my seat, Will's sitting in the seat beside mine and my plate's gone. "Give me my damn plate," I say in an exasperated tone, knowing he has hidden it. He pulls it out from his lap and puts it in front of me, snickering. "I was expecting to have to ask more than that. Are you tired or something?"

"Yeah, I am."

REED HAD CALLED AND LEFT a message during the day. I'd forgotten all about meeting him and his cousin Chip at the traveling fair in the Kmart parking lot. He wants me to come by his house and take him up on his offer to play some basketball. I don't see why not, so I go over. He lives around the country club and the rest of the rich people in town. So I go over to his house and shoot some roundball with him and Chip. There's a hoop set up over his garage. Beside the hoop there's a sign that reads MOVE OUT!

They're good, better than my friends at Central, but I can keep up. These are guys who go to clinics and basketball camps during the summer, taking their game to the next level. If I want to play varsity, I would have to do the same thing. Not to mention practice until seven or eight every night. It doesn't seem worth it. We play for a couple of hours and then sit around drinking Gatorade in Reed's spacious living room. It's got this vaulted ceiling that goes up about twenty feet.

"Samuel, you wanna come with us later? We're gonna have some fun," says Chip.

"What's the plan?" I ask.

"You don't have to come if you don't want. I'm not sure if I'm even gonna go," says Reed.

"Why the hell not?" asks Chip.

"I got Christina to think about," says Reed.

"What is it?" I ask.

"There's a girl who'll do it with all of us."

"You mean at the same time?"

"No, one at a time. That's why it's called a train. But I guess if you wanted . . ."

"What is she, some kind of hooker?" I ask.

"No, she just likes it."

"Is that normal?" I ask.

"She's just a crazy slut," says Reed.

"I don't know about Samuel, but you're definitely comin'," Chip says to Reed. "You wouldn't want Christina finding out about those other times . . ."

Reed looks at him like he's getting angry. "You don't want to go there, cuz."

They both stare at each other for a good minute. "Forget about it then, goddamnit!" says Chip, and starts playing a video game on the plasma television mounted on the wall between two large bookcases full of plates and statues. I tell them I'm heading out, and Chip says, "Yeah," without even turning from his game. Reed walks me out to the front door.

"Don't worry about him, Samuel. He's just pissed at me because I got a girlfriend and don't go slumming with him and his skanks. Take it easy."

I head home to find Dad already there working on his project. He's digging deeper into that hole in the backyard.

"You need any help?" I ask.

"Naw, son. I got to do this on my own." He wipes his forehead with a towel and looks up at the late-afternoon sky before digging again. He looks old but strong.

CHAPTER 11

MY COUSIN, ANGIE, WANTS TO SEE ME after school the next day. She said she wants to tell me something in person, and no matter how much I try to get her to tell me over the phone she refuses. Angie has just graduated from the West Georgian College and is substitute teaching at Sugweepo City High across town. We used to play together when we were kids, but the age gap caught up with us as she entered high school and then college. I don't feel like going. I'm all nervous and agitated for some reason. I keep having these little flashbacks with Daryl and that shed mixed in with those babies. It's like one of those watercolor paintings from the basement of Will's house. Impressions that bleed in on one another. I'd figure it would make me want to run for the hills, but instead it just makes me want to go to Mrs. Greenan's house more. Like I could do something to make it all stop, but I don't know what.

I call Angie on my cell phone. She tells me to go to the back of her school and park by the weight room, which is easier said than done. With school getting out it takes half an hour to get through the slew of students leaving and the parents coming to pick up their kids. Then when I try to park by the weight room, some coach blows a whistle and tells me to go back around and try to find a spot up front. I have to loop around three times before I find a spot. I walk around looking for room 122, which she said was in the far west side of the school. Angie's sitting behind a desk in the classroom. She looks like a genuine grown-up with a suit and a perm, but she still has that youngish oval face and round John Lennon glasses. She puts out her arms and grabs me by the shoulders. "There's something I need you to do for me. A friend of mine is getting married next week, and we're having a rehearsal and pictures this weekend. She needs a guy to be matched with one of the maids of honor. I need you to be a stand-in."

"Why me?" I ask.

"Because I know you're sweet, not to mention generous and intelligent . . ."

"Come on. You're saying you can't find one other guy around you who's willing to do this? What's the catch?"

"Look, I'll give you fifty dollars."

"Fifty dollars to walk down an aisle and have some pictures taken?"

"Yes."

"What about the actual wedding?"

"We have someone lined up for that. Just the rehearsal and the pictures." She takes out the fifty, and when she sees me hesitate she adds ten more. I take it. Stupid me. Stupid, because when I get home and tell Dad the rehearsal is in Heflin, he tells me Heflin is in Alabama, two hours away. That's why she wanted to see me in person. What with the bribe and the face-to-face contact, she knew I'd cave in. Dad offers to call Angie and tell her I can't make it, but I tell him it's too late. "Greed did me in," I say. "I said I'll do it, and I'll do it."

"Give Jim a call while you're going out in that direction," says Dad. The West Georgian College is about forty-five minutes west of Sugweepo, on the way toward Alabama.

"I think he wants to be left alone, Dad," I say. "I don't want to bother him."

"If he's bothered, it's not because of you, so don't even worry about that. You might even be able to help him out. Sometimes we need help when we don't even know it."

"I don't know, Dad," I say.

"Don't forget that you two are brothers. All right? Come on, let's order a pizza," he says.

I know I'll have to go do that favor for Angie that Saturday, so I make sure to go out that Friday night. Will comes by and picks me up to go to the mall, where we just cruise around for a while and then spend some time in the video arcade behind the movie theater. That's where we run into Joe, a.k.a. "Captain Crazy." Will knows Joe better than me because Joe used to be on the swim team. Maybe he still is. I'm not sure. There's a party he wants to go to but he doesn't want to go alone so he asks us if we want to go with him.

"Sure," says Will. I just follow along. We hop in Joe's red Trans Am and head out to Fairfield Plantation, a wealthy subdivision heading toward Atlanta, thirty miles northeast of Sugweepo. He drives around the hilly wooded suburbs, making phone calls and cursing, "Goddamnit! Where is this place! Shit! That lying piece of shit, giving me shit directions. Fuuuuaaaak!" But he just can't find it. "You know, I think the principal lives around here," he says ominously, while still driving around. He keeps punching his thigh with his right hand, which is gripping his cell phone.

"Oh shit! Is that a cop?" Will asks.

"Where?" asks Joe.

"That car keeps following us."

Joe slows down the car and starts cruising beside those large well-kept lawns.

"It doesn't look like a cop car," says Joe. "Let's see." He pulls into a random driveway, and we watch as a white Charger with blue stripes on the side passes. There's only one person that could be.

"Maybe we should just go home," I say. All the nervousness comes back in a wave of cold sweat that I feel in my armpits and on my forehead. "Shit. I got a bad feeling about this."

"Why? It wasn't even a cop. Come on," says Joe.

Will shrugs at me. "It wasn't a cop."

We back out of the driveway and continue winding around the labyrinthine suburbs searching for some stupid party. I keep looking for the Charger, hoping we've lost it.

"Let's just go," I plead. "We're not going to find it."

"Hey, it's still following us," says Will.

"You sure?"

"Yeah." We all look back and see a pair of headlights three or four car lengths behind us. Joe starts taking quick random turns.

"See, I told ya," says Will.

"I'll be damned. Who do you think it is?" asks Joe, peering into the rearview mirror.

"Does it matter? Let's just get the hell out of here!" I say.

"Well, if it ain't a cop, then it's got no right." Joe drives faster and faster. He even starts swerving off the road, into people's front yards, and back onto the road.

"What the hell are you doing, Joe?" Will asks. Joe pulls off the road completely and jumps the curb, driving through yards and dodging mailboxes, bushes, and trees without slowing down or turning back on the road. In fact, he's speeding up. Will and I look at each other. He shakes his head and puts on his seat belt. I do the same. But I have to say, at the moment I'm impressed with Joe's driving skills. I can't believe how he manages to avoid all those obstacles: lawn gnomes, trees, shrubs, pine-straw islands, all while maintaining control of a speeding car.

"He's still there!" yells Will.

"Just go!" I say. "Go! Go! Go!"

We reach a point where the road veers away to the right. It's Joe's last chance to get back on the road. He doesn't take it. Instead, he goes past a small pond, around a brick bird feeder, up this grassy hill, and into someone's backyard full tilt, and we slam into the side of a house, crashing through all these sliding-glass doors into a living room. Then it's quiet. Joe looks around and says, "Holy shit. This should be a tradition. We gotta find the principal's house and do this." He starts trying to back up, but the car is stuck against something. I can hear the car wheels squealing and smell the rubber burning. Somewhere in the house I hear a woman screaming.

I climb out of the car window onto a comfortable beige sofa and run out the gaping hole where the side of the house once was. Will's right behind me. "Split up!" I say, before turning toward the woods behind the house. Will heads left, and I see him disappear as he hurdles a line of hedges into someone else's backyard. I'm busting through the tree line into darkness. That's what it's like the first few minutes: racing through darkness. I'm just trying to avoid running into trees, but every other form of plant life— branches and bushes and brambles—are slapping and scraping me. I stop for a second to catch my breath and let my eyes adjust to the half-moon light. Shapes start to emerge. The inner forest appears before me in blurry silhouettes and shadows. I start running again but at a jogging pace, picking my way through the woods more deliberately. I'm sweating big time, and I can't help but think I hear another pair of footsteps. I stop to listen, but there're only crickets and frogs. And then I hear it: police sirens in the distance. I quicken my pace, veering back toward the direction of the main road. Imagination or not, I can't help stop thinking about him out there in the woods with me. It makes the cops seem a hell of a lot more pleasant. I keep running.

Eventually the brush clears, and I come upon an old log cabin in the middle of the woods. It's the kind of thing you might see on a bottle of maple syrup, some place Daniel Boone might have lived. I hear a vague whimper coming from inside, then a moan. I start jogging on by as quietly as I can. There's a trail leading away from the cabin, which I hope takes me back to a road. That's when some guys come out from the other side of the cabin with flashlights.

I start running hard down the trail, and I'm pretty fast. But these guys are damn faster. There're three of them, and that's plenty enough to beat the crap out of me. "Hey, stop!" says a familiar voice. I can't outrun them anyway. I'm too damn tired so I stop and turn. A light's flashed in my face.

"Samuel?" one of them says.

He flashes the light onto his own face. "It's me, Chip. What the hell are you doin' out here? Did Reed send you?" he asks. I'm breathing so hard I can barely talk.

"Cops . . ." I gasp, leaving Daryl out of the mix.

"Cops? Where?"

"They're probably coming . . ."

"Shit, what the hell happened?"

"We drove a car into a house. And there was some guy already following us."

They grab me and start running. At the end of the trail is a parked car. We all get in and drive to the end of the trail and onto a dirt road.

"What about Todd?" says one of the cronies to Chip.

"He'll be okay," Chip says, and we speed down the dirt road and onto a paved one, where we get on the highway past Fairfield Plantation.

"What were you guys doing back there?" I ask.

"That's where we bring the girl. Shit, there goes our night. What do you guys want to do?"

"Just drop me off at my house," I say, and start giving them directions.

"That's a good idea. Lay low."

They drop me off, and I station myself in front of my black-and-white TV for the rest of the night. My cell phone rings around eleven. It's Will calling from a gas station a few miles down from Fairfield. I tell Dad I have to give a ride to a friend who drank too much. He commends my lie.

When I pull up to the gas station, Will's sitting on the curb by the ice machine staring into space with a Gatorade in his hand. He's soaked with sweat.

"Are you okay?" I ask.

"I just ran almost six miles through the woods. What happened to you?"

So I tell him about Chip and the boys with their sex cabin.

"I guess they weren't rumors then," he says. "I wonder who it was. I heard Jenny Flynn was into that."

"Hell if I know."

I take him back to his car at the mall. Before separating, we make up a backstory about how we were watching a movie at the time of the house ramming, just in case Joe talks. I'm super careful driving home, making sure not to be followed. I keep checking the rearview. After I get home I go up on the roof and keep a lookout from under the stars. When Dad goes to bed, I give all the doors and windows a once-over, making sure to draw all the blinds. I take the hunting knife from under the mattress and slip it under my pillow before settling down to sleep.

CHAPTER 12

MY TEMPO JUST ISN'T RELIABLE ENOUGH for that long of a drive, so I leave for the wedding rehearsal out in Heflin, Alabama, at eleven-thirty in the morning that Saturday in Dad's car. I take one food break and one bathroom-stretch break at a gas station just beyond the West Georgian College, which sits halfway between Sugweepo and Heflin. I give Jim a call along the way but he doesn't answer so I leave a message telling him about the rehearsal and how I'm passing through and all. I'm not a hundred percent sure he'll call back, he being reclusive as he's been but at least I tried.

The rehearsal starts at three and is supposed to end a half hour to an hour later. Angie and the bride and her bridesmaids are already there by the time I get to the church. There're four of them: the bride-to-be, Terry, along with Julie and Angie and one younger girl, Naomi.

They gush all over how nice I look. I'm wearing a nice Polo dress shirt with a tie and have a jacket to go with it but it's way too hot for that. I've got a pair of jeans and running shorts along with other casual clothes in a gym bag for when it finishes.

Naomi's the one I came to be pictured with. Her boyfriend, Carl, refused to come. He's my brother's housemate at college, so she already knows a little about me. I can't tell what her race is, maybe a little Hispanic, I think. She definitely has the dark complexion for it, but her hair is almost blond-colored, which doesn't seem Hispanic to me. Not that it matters. She's pretty. And she has a tall, curvy body. Probably better than any girl at Sugweepo Central High. She even had ole Mrs. Baker beat.

"You don't look anything like your brother," she tells me.

I don't know what to say, so I blurt out, "I'm much smarter than him."

She gives me a quizzical smile. "Are you staying for the dinner afterward?"

"I don't know," I say. "I didn't know there was one."

"What's the name of that town you're from again?"

"Sugweepo. I think in Native American it means 'tangerine grove.'"

"You're kind of funny," she says.

The men show up together a little later. Angie's boyfriend, Mark, is there, and so is Terry's fiancé, Phil, and Julie's boyfriend, Tony. We take a ton of pictures, all the men, all the women, couples, every permutation imaginable. It seems to keep going forever. Then they end up having the rehearsal much later than anyone expects. While the rest are finishing up with some more pictures, I take a seat in the back of the church and check my messages. Jim called and actually invited me to visit and stay the night. He says later on in the evening I could come along with some of his buddies to hit some bars. It'd be the first time we've done anything in a long time. Now I want this wedding gig to hurry up and end.

Naomi comes over and sits down beside me. "It's almost over," she encourages me, with a pat on the back.

"How do you know these guys?" I ask.

"Terry's a second cousin. We lived close to each other when she was in New York."

"You're from New York?"

"I'm a Brooklyn girl."

"You're the way I imagined a Brooklyn girl would look like."

"And how do I look?"

"Kind of mixed-up."

She laughs. "Mixed-up, huh? I guess maybe I am, come to think of it."

"I didn't mean that in a bad way. I love mixed . . . things."

"Yeah, yeah, yeah."

"No, I mean it. You actually remind me of a friend from school."

"Is she pretty?" she smiles.

"Very."

"So you know everyone here?"

"Yeah, I know everyone here except Terry and Phil. But they seem okay."

"What about Julie?"

"I know her through Angie. She's a little sneaky," I say. Naomi seems pleased with what I say, so I continue. "What I mean by sneaky is, a couple years ago she promised to take me on a road trip she was going to go on. I was all excited and had a bag packed and everything. Then when I saw her that summer, she had asked some girlfriend to go with her instead, because I didn't respond to her e-mail, which was a lie. I was the last one to send her an e-mail. I didn't say anything, but I knew she was full of it. I used to think she was pretty."

"How old are you, Samuel?"

"Sixteen."

"Sixteen," she says wistfully.

"How old are you?"

"Twenty."

"That's kinda old."

She laughs. "Tell me about it."

"Well, not that old. Hell, it's just four years."

"That's very sweet of you to say."

Tony and Julie sit down on the other side of the pew. Tony's got a briefcase full of papers. He's a graduate student studying psychology. He's a nice guy, so I don't understand what he's doing with Julie. She's kind of pretty, with long brunette hair, but like I said to Naomi, she's a sneak.

"Listen to the stuff this guy is writing," says Julie.

She starts reading, " 'Both males and females experience orgasms, but the exact response varies depending on sex. Generally speaking, orgasm is the third stage of four in the human sexual response cycle, which is the currently accepted model of the physiological process of sexual stimulation. Even infants as young as five months are capable of experiencing orgasm, as documented in the research of Alfred Kinsey.' This is what his paper is on. This is science," she says sarcastically.

"Don't listen to her. She's frigid."

"Samuel, do you cum?" she asks in a fake scientist's voice. They both crack up over that. My face had already started getting a little red, but now I can feel it turning warm soon to be hot. I can see them noticing my redness.

Before it becomes a ridicule-Samuel-fest, I turn on the humor, and in my best snooty Englishman's voice, I say, "Of course not, but instead of 'Do you cum' don't you mean, in scientific terms, 'Do you climax?' " I say. They both laugh at that, and I've successfully deflected a potential barrage. That's when I realize why I had liked Julie in the first place. She usually pretends to be prim and proper when she's around people she doesn't know, but when she knows you, she shows her natural dirty side. I guess Tony can look past the sneaky part.

When it's all over, I tell them about my meeting Jim and how sorry I am for skipping out on the dinner. We say our good-byes and I head back east into Georgia toward the West Georgian College.

JIM'S APARTMENT IS AT THE very top of a three-story brick building fifteen minutes from the college. It sits in between a row of short office buildings. I go up a set of white narrow stairs on the side with no handrail to the third floor and knock on the door there. Jim opens the door in his boxers. He looks like he just woke up: serious bed head and bushy eyes. He was already stout, but now he's entering the pudgy zone. "Hey, bro, come in," he says. Inside Jim's two-bedroom apartment there're papers and notebooks and files all over the kitchen table. And there're more on the coffee table in front of the sofa. Pretty much every flat surface has something on it. "I've been up for almost forty-eight hours, bro. I gotta get some sleep before we go out. You can watch some TV." He goes in his room and shuts the door. I look around for Carl. Luckily he isn't there. I have the place to myself, so to speak, seeing as how Jim's in the sack. I turn on the TV and plop down on the sofa. There's some political news program on. I can't find the remote, and I don't feel like getting up, so I slip off my shoes and lie back. Even though it's boring as hell, I can't remember feeling so relaxed in weeks. It's a nice feeling and one that I don't want to lose. It doesn't feel like there's another darker world out there, just this one, with one real me. On the TV, an Asian woman's interviewing two guests: a big old college professor wearing a brown tweed jacket with a red tie and a skinny young journalist with a white shirt and tie on.

The old professor begins blabbing about the cold war and Reagan. When the young man tries to say something, the old professor asks him, "Now what have you gotten published?"

The skinny journalist stutters, "I-I-I don't have to explain myself to you." Geez, I think I wonder if I ever sound like that. Daryl sure the hell made me feel that way. The old professor tells the journalist that if he hasn't published any books, he shouldn't be on that show. The young journalist stutters some more and gets red in the face. I stick my hand between the cushions and find the remote down there. I turn to a basketball game and find myself saying, "Ahhhhh," like I'm lying down in a hot bubble bath.

Jim gets up a little past nine and throws a frozen pizza in the oven for our dinner while he gets a shower. Then we have our pizza in front of the TV. I want to ask him about something. Something I've been thinking about off and on. Like I said, he was the last one to be with our mom before she couldn't even talk anymore. We just don't talk about it. But still, it seems like she would have said something. Anything. When Jim finally says something, it's to ask me about school. "So when does summer vacation officially start?"

"About two weeks left," I say.

"You got any plans?"

"I guess work at the store. I don't know."

"How about doing something for me? I've been working extra hours at my part-time job, and I'm barely getting by at school. I might have to miss a couple classes, but if I do I think I might flunk out. Just to be safe, how's about sitting in on a few classes for me. Just for a week or two until final exams. It'd just be taking notes—classes in big auditoriums or labs, you'd need to show your student ID, and all this other stuff. Don't worry. It's just a couple classes."

"Can't you get off work for your classes?"

"I need this job or I can't even afford school, period."

"If you miss those classes, you're sure you're going to flunk out?"

"I'm not a hundred percent sure. It's just that some of them have mandatory attendance. Look, if you don't want to do it, that's fine. I should be okay."

"No, I should be able to."

We watch some TV together, and it feels like old times back at home. It feels good. Jim's buddies, Chang and Jason, show up soon after. Jason's a Floridian who's spent a couple years in the navy before moving to Georgia. He's real thin and has the face of a famous young actor who died a few years ago from a drug overdose. "No Carl tonight?" Jason asks.

"No Carl," says Jim.

"Thank you, Lord," Jason says, with palms pressed together. Chang's on his cell phone almost the entire time, talking to his Korean girlfriend in Korea. Chang isn't Korean though. He's Chinese, and his hair goes down his back in a ponytail. He's almost as pudgy as Jim. We all get in Jason's Bronco and head into town.

"You don't have a fake ID, do you?" Jason asks me.

"Nah, he doesn't," says Jim. He turns around. "Do you?"

"No," I say.

"I know a place. If the guy I know is carding, you should be good."

Chang's still talking to that girl. "No, I'm not angry, just disappointed. Well, I didn't get that e-mail . . ."

We cruise around for a time looking for a parking space downtown. It's hard because there're plenty of cars doing the same thing we are. Once we find someone backing up, we pull up and get our spot. Then it's off to a bar called the Pioneer, a dive-looking place in between some restaurants. Jason goes in first. He pokes his head back out and says, "It's cool."

I follow Jim and Chang into a dark smoky bar tinted red from the neon signs behind the counter, which lines the left side. On the right are tables and booths, which are packed. I can't tell which is louder, the rock music or all the people trying to talk over the music in such a small space. My brother and Chang show their driver's licenses to this curly-haired tough guy sitting on a stool, who then stamps their wrists. I start to take out mine when Jason says, "He's with us."

The curly-haired guy nods and stamps me. I follow the guys through the sea of people to the back. Jason sits us down at a booth at the very end of the bar. Chang's yelling into his cell phone the whole time. "I'm in a bar! No, no, I said I'm in a bar!"

"Samuel, that guy at the door?" says Jason.

"Yeah."

"Guys like him are bitches. They look tough, but all you got to do is slap them down one time, just one time, and then they show the kind of bitch they are. Remember that."

We all get beers. Chang's still on his phone. Jason and Jim are talking about work and school. It turns out Jason isn't even a student. He just lives there. Come to think of it, he really doesn't seem like a student. He's too tough, like he's been in quite a few fights. Even the way he dresses, he wears a sleeveless wife beater with a white jacket over it. He and my brother occasionally get up and talk to girls and then come back. I'm sitting with Chang drinking my second beer when a fight starts right in front of us. A big militant-looking guy has a guy who's wearing a dress shirt and necktie in a headlock. The necktie guy slips out and tackles the bigger guy, and they fall out of sight into the hallway that leads to the bathroom. That cold feeling in my gut comes back. Seeing those two guys fight makes me think of Daryl kicking the shit out of me. I hear Chang saying, "Oh, there's a fight. You wanna hear two guys fighting in a bar?" He places his cell phone faceup on the table. As this is happening a bearded guy with a big gut and a flannel shirt stands by our table and keeps looking at Chang. I can't figure out why. Chang doesn't seem to notice. He picks his cell phone up and says, "Hello? Hello? Shit!" Then he finally hangs up the phone. "Man, she's boring," he says.

Then Jason comes back and sits down. "Hey, you don't want to do that," Jason says to the bearded guy.

"I want to fight him," says the bearded guy, pointing at Chang.

"Me? Why me?" asks Chang, when he finally catches on.

"You talking on the cell phone is bothering me."

"It's a bar. Can you actually hear me on my cell phone?"

"You're Asian."

"Why do you want to fight an Asian?" asks Chang.

"I don't like Asians."

"What has an Asian ever done to you?"

"Nothing. But I just don't like them."

"They're productive members of society. Most stereotypes are of hardworking and industrious. Look, I'm not even the only one here." Chang points to some Asian guys and girls at a table. Then his phone rings, and he says, "Sorry, I have to get this. Hello? Sorry, but the line kept breaking up! Yeah, I know, I know."

The bearded guy walks away, and I feel better. But there's a part of me that would have liked to see Jason fight him. Jason tells me, "Samuel, just remember, if you ever get in a fight, just keep getting back up and fighting, even if they're dragging you all around the parking lot bleeding and screaming. You keep fighting; they'll give up. That means you win."

On the television mounted behind the bar wall there's a movie showing a samurai fighting big green shiny beetles on some planet that doesn't look like the Earth. The clip ends, and it shows people dressed up as those beetles in that movie. It's an advertisement for a local anime exposition. Then it goes back to a baseball game.

As the night goes on Jason eventually meets a dark-haired Russian girl who invites all of us to a party she's going to. She asks us to walk her and her blond friend to their car first, so we follow them across the street out to the bank parking lot. At the end of the parking lot is a fence with a gate that swings open. All the guys go through, and then for the fun of it I run up and swing it open as hard as I can. It opens all the way, letting the girls walk through.

"Thank you," they say with smiles.

Their car's on the other side of the fence, so Jim and Chang stay with them while Jason and me go back to retrieve their car. We follow them in her Camry out of town to a house in the suburbs, where we park on the street along with dozens of other cars. Once we get inside everyone scatters and seems to disappear in a matter of moments, and it's just me and a bunch of strangers. It's just like the bar except in a living room. Jim reappears a moment later with a beer in his hand.

"Bro, do you think you could drive us back?"

"Sure," I say.

"Thanks, man," he pats me on the back. Jason comes back and puts a pack of cigarettes in my pocket.

"I don't smoke," I say.

"Designated driver needs a bad habit," he says. He follows the dark-haired Russian girl to a sofa, where she straddles him and starts kissing him. *What the hell? How does that happen?* I wonder. I feel pretty damn stupid standing there, so I find a wall to lean against. I take out the pack Jason gave me and find a girl who's smoking.

"Do you have a light?" I ask.

She lights my cigarette, and I take some small puffs. I've tried smoking once before and nearly coughed my lungs up, so I know to take it slow. It makes me feel a little dizzy, so I just kind of hold it without puffing. After a while I notice the cigarette has gone out so I ask the girl for a light again.

"You're gonna burn yourself," she says with a smile.

"It'll be all right," I say.

She's right. The cigarette's too short, and when I puff the flame goes right at my mouth. "Are you okay?" she asks.

"That was pretty dumb," I say, and walk off to the bathroom, where I check my lip in the mirror. There's no blister or burn. It looks normal, just a typical unassuming mouth, but when I touch it, it stings. I open and close it, feeling the slight pain when my upper lip stretches. It looks like I'm talking without making a sound. Hell, I think. There's no such thing as a perfect mouth. Only on something so imperfect everywhere else would it seem so. How else would those baby mouths look like that? Their mouths were normal not perfect. They didn't even say anything, just opened and closed like a fish trying to breath out of water. But it looked like they were trying to talk. What could something like that possibly say? It'd be like a fish talking. I look at myself for a long while. I can't say I remember ever doing that, staring at myself like that. It's a weird feeling. The more I stare, the less I recognize the face in the mirror. It could be anyone. The skin and flesh, the eyes and nose, it's all some kind of crapshoot. Those babies are just a part of the same crapshoot that made me. That made Daryl. I notice I feel kind of hot. Am I getting a fever? I check my forehead. It feels cool and damp. Then someone comes in the bathroom, and I get out in a rush. I wade through the party people to the kitchen in search of coffee, something to kill the fatigue. Once I get in there, I nod to the handful of people there and start checking out the pantries when some shaggy-haired stranger wearing a blue flannel shirt asks, "What're you doin'?"

"Is there any coffee?" I ask.

"Coffee?"

"Designated driver."

"Sorry to hear that." He opens the freezer for me. "Help yourself." There's a pack of some French coffee called Crème de la Busche. So not having anything to do, not knowing anyone there, I make coffee. I watch it percolating, and then drip into the coffeepot. And I listen to the people in the kitchen. They watch me making coffee and talk. One guy's talking about how he burned a small barn full of marijuana. "It was a small barn behind my girlfriend's house. I don't know why we did it. I guess me and my buddies thought it would be funny?"

"Funny? It's not funny in jail."

"No jail time, man."

"What? They didn't catch you?"

"After we got it burning we all ran in different directions. I pretended to be jogging, but some cops caught me anyway. But no jail time."

The strong smell of French coffee wafts from the kitchen into the rest of the house. People come to see what the smell is. Some want a cup, especially those who have to drive back home like me. I make a second pot and am dubbed the "coffee guy."

I'm sipping on a cup of coffee listening to a story about a guy who got on a school bus full of middle-school kids. The bus driver was his friend and offered to drop him by his girlfriend's house. During the ride the kids on the bus slowly turned against him and started harassing him. It started with asking him questions about who he was and what he was doing on their bus, next thing he knows they were throwing things at him, paper clips, pencils—whatever their little hands could grab. In the commotion they even threw his books out the window of the moving bus. The bus driver had to stop the bus so he could get his books. Some of the kids took pity on him and helped him pick up his things. Then he sat up front with his bus driver friend the rest of the way. Chang comes in the kitchen and says, "There you are! Are you ready? The rest of the guys are waiting in the living room." Chang takes me out to the living room and announces, "He's the coffee guy!"

"Ahhhh! Holy shit!" says Jim.

"Coffee man! Your brother's the coffee man!"

They grab me and take me back to the car. They're all drunkenly ranting and raving at cross-purposes while trying to navigate me back to the apartment. I make my way out of the subdivision onto the main roads into town. Soon I recognize Jim's apartment on the rise. As we pull up, someone with a laundry bag over one shoulder is locking Jim's apartment. We get out of the car, and Jim yells up, "What're you doing?"

It's a tall guy with blond close-cropped hair and wearing red-and-white warm-up clothes. I could see him being a white rapper. This guy who looks like a white rapper stops on the stairs and brings his pinched fingers to his puckered lips before going on the second-floor landing and walking over to the door to the apartment below.

"What an idiot. He thinks he's a gangster," Jason whispers. "He's gonna get himself in trouble one day because he's so goddamn stupid."

"He got us a hell of a deal on our apartment, man," says Jim.

"Is it worth it having a drug-dealing landlord living right under your feet?"

"He told me, once we got the place, we wouldn't have to deal with the landlord."

"Yeah, except once a week when Carl goes to buy all that weed from him. The moron just doesn't get it. I'm going home. Chang, you want a ride?"

"Just crash here tonight, man. What if you get pulled over?"

"I'll take my chances with the cops rather than with that bastard."

Chang finally chimes in, "Dude, you need to dump that asshole. He's gonna bring you down." Chang gets in the Bronco with Jason and they drive off. A Mexican lady opens the door on the second floor, and the guy who I assume is Carl goes inside. We go up the stairs to Jim's, where I crash in Carl's room. The coffee keeps me awake for a while and I just lay there. I can hear Carl and that Mexican woman arguing from downstairs. Carl gets extra loud, and I can hear him saying, "Listen to this scenario, okay! Listen to this scenario!" Then it gets quiet. Eventually I hear the door slam and I'm worried Carl will come back up here, but he doesn't. His room smells like cologne, and on the walls there're a lot of posters of women in bikinis and lingerie. On a shelf are two identical rubber masks that look like fleshy caricatures of angry maniacal men. Both have mustaches. The two identical faces stare at me through the dark. I close my eyes and after some time fall asleep and dream . . .

. . . I'M WORKING ON A very high-tech offshore oil rig out in the Gulf of Mexico. This little platform surrounded by miles and miles of water. It looks futuristic, all metal and smooth lines. Almost everything's done by computers and robots. I head a crew of five men who make sure each sector they're in charge of is running smoothly. Then one day the rig is taken over by an evil force. It's those two fleshy masks from Carl's room . . .

It scares me so bad it wakes me up. I take some of those blankets off the bed and crash on the couch in the living room.

I GET UP AROUND EIGHT. Jim's still in bed and there's no telling how long he'll be in there and I don't want to bug him, so I get up and head on out, making sure to leave a note of thanks on his fridge. It's a long and lonely drive home, and I feel tired and empty. The closer I get to Sug-weepo, the closer Daryl gets in my thoughts. I really hope that cat he wanted me to kill got away. Just thinking about it turns my stomach.

By the time I get to Sugweepo I'm sure I got a fever. I just want to lie down on my back and forget I was even born, but I keep driv-ing. As I cruise through town I see the Kmart up ahead, and I'm reminded of what's lurking in the woods back there. Even though it feels like the whole thing is some out-of-control monster waiting beneath the surface of things, there's a small part of me that feels like I can do something about it, a little nugget of anger that wasn't there before. And it's just enough to get me to turn into the Kmart and drive to the back lot. That goddamn shed. If there're any of those animals there, I'm going to set them free. I drive by the garbage bin, making sure the Charger's not there. Then I drive to the front lot and park along with the few Sunday shoppers. I walk back, past the Dump-sters, and start down the dirt path then cut through a large patch of kudzu that leads into the woods. It's nice and peaceful in there, and I have to remind myself what I'm doing, what's really in there. Ten minutes come and go as I'm walking through the brush. It'll take at least thirty minutes if I keep that pace so I start jogging. The clearing is the same as before—shed set against the red dirt ridge, a fence on one side—but the cages are gone. I toss a rock at the shed from a dis-tance just to make sure no one's in there then peek inside. It's empty. On the bloodstained workbench are three of those hinged boxes with the holes at the top laid out in a row. No animals, so I turn and start running back down the path, occasionally stopping to listen for ap-proaching footsteps. By the time I get back to my car and am heading home, I'm soaked in a cold sweat.

I tell Dad I've come down with a fever and go straight to bed. I can hear him in the backyard building that installation art that Mom designed. He's really going through with it. The man without an artistic bone in his body. I can even hear him whistling while he works. He sounds happy. There's only the wall of the house separating us, but it feels like he's in a completely other world. On a different planet. One with sunshine and good hard work and whistling. I'm the alien in that world. I'm the two-headed fetus floating in formaldehyde. I wish I could become a part of his world. I wish I had something to do to make me whistle. Something that would make me forget everything.

CHAPTER 13

I'M STILL FEELING COLD AND CLAMMY on Monday. Dad tells me just to stay home, but I have to go to school because it's the day a volunteer group of us students go to Sugweepo Elementary School for a visit. Among our group one of us has to assist in teaching twice a week for three months. I taught the previous three months, and it's my duty to visit my old students this time around. It's going to look good on my college application.

I sit through my morning classes, and then around lunchtime Clay, Will, Sheri, and I take a school minivan to the elementary school. Dad was right about me staying at home. My fever's just getting worse, and those crazy eight- and nine-year-olds aren't going to help the situation. The only reason they liked me as a teacher was because I played games with them all the time. I even played touch football with them in the hallway one day when it was raining. I got in trouble for that one.

When we get there we're met by Ted, one of the teachers I got to know during my stint there. He was once a marine and now a bit of a blowhard, but for the most part he's okay, even though most of the time I don't think he knows what the hell he's talking about. He has a bunch of sack lunches, which he hands out to us.

"Samuel, come back for a job?" he asks.

"Not on your life."

"You know you loved those kids. I was always watching you."

"Meh," I say.

"Ha-ha. Samuel, could you take your group to the classroom while I get some Cokes for your lunch?"

"Sure."

We walk over to the assistant-teacher classroom. Along the way in the hall I see familiar kids who weren't my students but who recognize me anyway. They say, "Hello!"

I say, "Hi."

I stop my group on an inclined walkway, from where we can look into the classroom. Down on the ground floor the classroom door is open and Lizard's talking to the students. Lizard is Christa, a tall blond girl we call Lizard because of her skinniness and stooped-over posture. She has inherited my third-grade class, and from what I've heard has quickly become popular with the kids. We lean against a railing and start eating our lunches, peanut butter jelly sandwiches wrapped in plastic wax paper.

"This lunch sucks big time," says Will. There's some grape jelly oozing out of the corner of his sandwich. That jelly makes me a little nervous. Will is too unpredictable for not only his but everyone else's good, especially mine. Lizard stops teaching for a minute and waves at us. All the kids then come to the door and wave, too. Lizard's apparently told them we're visiting because some of the students made a sign reading "We love you, Samuel!"

"Samuel!" says some of the kids. "We love you!" They yell up to me in their high childish nine-year-old voices. I can't believe it.

"You don't even know me," I say off the top of my head.

"Hey, Samuel, you can have some of my sandwich," says Will.

As soon as he says that I start ducking my head. But it's too late. He's taken some of that jelly and rubs it in my face, laughing that goofy laugh of his. I try to grab it from him, but he pulls away. I manage to get a piece of it and smear it in his face. All the while he's trying to smear more on mine. It's really pissing me off. He starts backing away from me, still laughing, but his back hits the railing. "I got you now, bastard," I say as I start choking him with both hands. He's too surprised to react. His face gets red, and he just looks at me with astonished eyes. Then while choking him with my left hand I take my right and start smearing the sandwich around his mouth. I even try to shove it down his throat.

In the distance it sounds like someone's calling me, a woman's voice from far away. "Samuel! Samuel!" It becomes louder and louder and there are other voices, too.

"Samuel, stop."

"Let him go!"

I let go with my shaking hands. Will's coughing and spitting up a mixture of bread and saliva.

"I'm sorry," I say, taking deep breaths. "You can choke me back if you want."

I walk over to a bench and sit down. He comes over and sits beside me without saying a word. My hands are shaking again, so I put them in my pockets.

"Samuel, what's wrong with you?" asks Sheri. They all seem confused and concerned.

"I don't know."

Ted comes back from wherever he was and sees something has

happened. "They got in a fight," says Sheri. "Will put jam on Samuel's face, and Samuel choked him for it."

"I was just playing," says Will.

Ted sits down beside me and begins lecturing me, "You need to slow down, Samuel. You have too many high expectations about yourself. I could see that when you were here. You're just going to drive yourself crazy that way. Just slow it down. Look at me," he says, with his hands out. "I'm an old man, but I'm healthy. I just became head teacher. I know things."

Will has a very confused look on his face while Ted's giving one of his I'm-old-so-I-know-everything, blowhard spiels. I just nod my head, hoping he'll go away. Then a plastic red ball with a face painted on it lands in between Will and me. Then a blue one comes down on Ted's head.

"You're dead," a child's voice says from below. Then colorful plastic balls start falling all over us. We're being pelted from below by Lizard's students. Ted and the rest of the guys get out of the way, as if they know we have it coming to us. Will and I just sit there getting bombarded. When they run out of those balls, they start throwing plastic inflatable cars and trucks that actually sting when they hit. Will and I dodge those while slowly slinking down the ramp until we reach some doors that lead out to an open yard of grass that slopes down to a playground.

"What the hell was Ted talking about back there?" Will asks.

"He's always like that. Just nod your head enough, and he goes away. Well, we should probably help clean up those toys."

"Yeah."

"I need to make a phone call first. Could you give me a minute?"

"Sure, but I'm not cleaning alone."

Will goes back in, and I take out my cell phone. My hands are steady enough to make a call to Melody. I just want to talk to her for some reason. She doesn't answer, so I leave a message asking her to call me back, and then go inside to help clean up. All the little kids come out and scold Will and me for fighting. "No fighting!"

"You don't fight."

"Didn't your momma teach you not to fight?"

They continue reprimanding us for a while and then they help us pick up the toys. It turns out that when the little kids saw us fighting and Lizard saw how upset they were, she told them to unleash the rain of plastic balls, trains, and cars as a punishment, and they gladly did so. Like I said before, we had it coming to us.

CHAPTER 14

MELODY DOESN'T CALL ME BACK that day or for the next few days. It's not like her at all, so I drive to her house after school in the middle of the week. Her dad comes to the door. He's got a close-cropped Afro and thick mustache. He's looking quite angry.

"Is Melody in?" I ask.

"Who are you?"

"Samuel. I'm a friend of Melody."

His stern appearance softens somewhat. "The kid with the black-and-white television."

"I really appreciated your fixing that for me. Sorry it took me so long to pick it up."

"Don't worry about that. It was easy. I just can't believe you watch that thing. I can say you're the only person who's ever brought in a tiny black-and-white television."

s a kid, so it has some good

ore sense. You wanna come

I think he might regain
n spending a lot of time
?"

en I remember the tall
on our bike ride from

...na see her soon?" he asks me.

...est with you, sir, I don't know. But I'd like to."

"If you see her, could you tell her to stop by home? I've got something to give her," he says.

"Yes, sir."

I get in my car and head for the east side of town. My car starts making that grinding sound again, but luckily it goes away. I take it real slow when I reach the other side of the railroad tracks. I get a lot of stares by the passersby.

"You gonna get yaself killed driving around like that," someone yells.

"You know where Eric lives?" I yell back.

"Redmond or Tate?" says a well-built black guy wearing a black tank top.

"The young skinny one with the braces."

"Ah, he live up the street." He points. "Hang a right on Burnside, look for the house with the bed on the porch."

"Thanks."

Burnside's just up a couple blocks, past that building where I watched the fake animal documentary with the old man that time I was with Melody. I turn right and slow because I see the large queen-size bed. And it's on the porch, just like he said. There're some people lying on it while on one edge two people sit playing cards. I stop for a minute in front of the house to have a closer look. It's Eric and Melody lying there napping. They're fully clothed lying side by side, but he's much lower on the bed, with his feet curled up under him, and his head at Melody's stomach. It makes her seem maternal to me somehow. The two black girls playing cards don't seem to care about the day sleepers. Then a large muscular white man with no shirt comes out of the house with a haggard-looking black lady. They're greeting an old black guy with a big Afro coming from next door. They turn to toward me and start pointing, so I get out of there. I drive to Underwood with no idea what I want to do, but I need to do something. I just drive by and back around again before going home. After a hot shower I turn on my black-and-white television and get an idea. I sit down and write a letter:

> *Daryl plans on killing your babies. He's been hurting them. If you don't believe me, check their bodies for small bruises and marks. Maybe you've seen them already. It is him. He's a sadistic, evil man. He calls the babies monsters, freaks. He hates them. Save them.*

Then I practice saying it: "Daryl plans on killing your babies . . ." I whisper. No, "Daryl plans on killing your babies . . ." I say with a deep voice. No matter what, it sounds ridiculous. To hell with it, I resign myself to sounding stupid and drive out to the 7-Eleven. I've never used the pay phone there, but I've seen people on that thing. On the plastic shelf beneath the phone box I take out the chained phone book and look up Greenan at Underwood and find Doris Greenan, 770-834-6921. I call the number but hang up a couple times before I can muster up the courage actually to wait for an answer. But no one answers. I go in the 7-Eleven and buy a cherry slushy that I drink in my Tempo while watching the traffic and the self car wash across the street. After I finish my slushy I call again, and Daryl picks up. I hang up before he even finishes saying, "Hell . . ."

That night after dinner I tell Dad I'm going out to meet friends, but I go back to the 7-Eleven and call again. Mrs. Greenan finally says, "Hello."

I speak with the lowest voice I can, "Doris?" I try to sound like a big black man.

"That's me."

"Daryl plans on killing your babies. He's been—"

"What?"

"He's been hurting them. If you don't believe me, check their bodies for small bruises and marks . . ."

"Who the hell is this?"

"Maybe you've seen them already. It is him. He is a sadistic, evil man," I read in a deep monotone voice.

"Is this some kind of prank?"

"Listen! Shut up and listen to me!"

I wait for her to interrupt or say something, but she doesn't say anything so I continue, "Daryl plans on killing your babies. He's been hurting them. If you don't believe me, check their bodies for small bruises and marks. Maybe you've seen them already. It is him. He is a sadistic, evil man. He calls the babies monsters, demons. He hates them. Save them. Okay? Do you understand?"

"Go to hell. He wouldn't do that. He's their brother." I can hear her swallow down a sigh. I think she might be crying.

"You know," I say.

"I don't know what you're talking about. You lie. You're a god-damn liar."

"If you don't believe me, check their bodies."

"Who is this? Goddamnit!" she says hysterically.

I can't get myself to hang up, though I should have. "God," I say, and I hang up. I'm not trying to be funny or anything. It just came out. I get back in my car and sit there for a while watching traffic go by, my duty fulfilled. "I've done something about it. I've done my part," I say out loud to no one. "Now leave me the hell alone . . ."

CHAPTER 15

AS THE END OF THE SCHOOL YEAR APPROACHES a nauseous feeling comes over me, and my guts feel cold all the damn time. I wake up from nightmares I can't remember. And the light, the light feels dim. Even if it's sunny without a cloud in the sky, the light feels dimmed out. It's like twilight all the time, twenty-four hours a day. I know it's got to be in my mind, but there's nothing I can do about it. I'm tired all the time and constantly in a bad mood. I don't feel like riding my bike anymore. Not to mention my car is making that grinding noise again, so Dad has to give me a ride and pick me back up from school every day. I don't want to be a complete jerk to everyone, so I just keep to myself most of the time. When I do have to interact with people, I'm my old self but it's like I'm acting. Even my favorite television show depresses me. It's the one about the guys trapped in the desert town, *Devil in the Desert*, that comes on during the week but it has gotten so popular they stick it on Saturday night. I try to focus on studying for the final exams. When I keep my mind on only one thing like that, I feel kind of normal. And I do that up to the last day of school.

MY LAST TWO FINAL EXAMS finish early in the afternoon on Friday. Jamie, a guy I know from biology, knows about me going off school grounds to eat all the time and is trying to convince me to go out with him. I just want him to go away. I'm hardly even friends with the guy. "Let's check and see what we're having first," I say.

We go over to the cafeteria and peek at the food on the trays. It's some kind of turkey club sandwich with these big fish-eyed-looking black olives in there. "Look, the line is short, and I don't feel like walkin'," I say. He doesn't want to go alone so he gets in line with me. If Jamie hadn't been with me, I would have gone to the storage area behind the kitchen. I'd been going there for the past few days. The coaches and janitors didn't seem to mind as long as I stayed quiet. It made me feel calm eating lunch in there between those tall shelves instead of in the noisy cafeteria. I go ahead and eat with Jamie in the cafeteria like everyone else. His pasty white skin bugs me. Afterward I ditch him and go to the library to get some last-minute cramming in.

I thought I was ready for my algebra exam. In fact, I am, until I get to the last two questions. The anxiety of my next final exam, which is a presentation, begins slowly to invade my mind and melt into my thoughts. I start to sweat. I can't think straight. I keep reading the question over and over, but it doesn't make sense. It reads like this to me:

If one person is some fraction 100/245 and spends time with another person, what is the fraction of the third person?

No, I can't be reading that right. Impossible. No matter how many times I read it, it doesn't make sense. I end up just plugging the numbers into a formula Mrs. Easton gave. I get an answer and move on to the next question, but I'm still distracted by the thought of the presentation. If I finish this exam early, I might have more time to get ready. On to the last question, which is about the trajectory of a basketball in relation to tangential hand motions, requiring the actual cutting out of the basketball from the test paper. *Bullshit,* I think to myself. I'm losing my mind. I turn in my exam and sit back down. Even if I blew the last two questions I would still be all right as long as I had gotten the rest of the questions. I want to work on my next final but can't think straight, so I just sit there until time runs out.

The twenty-minute presentation I have to give for my final exam in world history is about the code of the Japanese samurai and its relation to contemporary Japan. I've done quite a bit of research and preparation. The problem is, when I get up in front of the teacher, I get dizzy and my mind goes blank. I rely completely on my note cards to get me through the next twenty minutes. I don't even know what I'm doing or saying. After I finish I can't remember a thing except having wiped sweat off my forehead and Mr. Bennett asking me if I was all right. I believe I responded by saying, "I was a little nervous." It was all like a blur.

When it's all over, I ask Mr. Bennett if I failed. He sits there a minute tabulating some numbers on his notepad. Mr. Bennett's a short, balding guy with a permanent five o'clock shadow. His pants seem to be too big all the time, and he walks around like a knocked-kneed butterball. But he's okay. He treats students fairly and seems to know his stuff.

"I'm going to give you a B minus, Samuel," he says, as if he wants to give me a higher grade but can't do it. "Your research was fine but the presentation killed you. You didn't look up from your note cards, not once." I don't care, but he goes on to give me some pointers on giving a speech, namely making eye contact and being engaging. Then I leave. My sophomore year is over. I go to my locker and clear out the few books that are left in there. I place the lock and the form with my picture on the top shelf. I'm finished, and the halls are still empty. It's only two-thirty in the afternoon, still a half hour before the chaos of the end of the school year officially ensues.

ALL I HAVE LEFT TO do is clean out my art class shelf. Actually, I really don't have to do that, because I take art every year and use the same shelf. But there's some stuff I want to get. When I exit the main building to go to the auditorium, I'm met with a steady drizzle of rain. The auditorium is almost always empty, except when the art or drama class is using it, so its main purpose is as a shortcut for students going to the art room. I go in expecting empty seats and find myself in the middle of a standing-room-only class being taught by Mrs. Busby. I can't just walk through while she's lecturing, so I sit down beside some students whose faces I kind of know. That's when I realize it's the school band. They're going to New York to compete in some band contest. It had been announced over the daily intercom, and I've seen flyers around school for the past month. They must be shipping off that day. All along the walls and the back are backpacks and traveling gear. It seems like some big pep rally before the send-off.

Mrs. Busby, with her gray beehive hair, asks the color guard to come out, and they do, dressed in their glittery tights. They file out in two lines on the right and left of the stage. Mrs. Busby asks the audience if any of them saw the famous University of Southern California marching band performance that was on television a couple of weeks ago, and some of the students raise their hands. "I want you to perform like that. Just like that!" she says. I'm busy looking at the color guard. There's one in particular, the prettiest one, who looks like she has silver eyes from where I sit. I want to get a closer look, so I move to a seat closer to the front. Her eyes are, in fact, blue. It must have been the silver-and-blue sequins on her tights messing with my eyes.

They start passing around these yellow flyers. The band people sitting in front of me deliberately pass it around me, knowing that I'm not one of them. Mrs. Busby announces the fliers are a list of other schools performing at the competition. Then she asks the audience if they're ready to perform. "Are you ready?" Mrs. Busby yells. "Are you ready to go up there and perform? Julie?"

"Yes, ma'am," a voice from up front says.

"Are you sure you're ready to perform?"

"Yes, ma'am!" the voice says louder, and then Julie comes up on stage.

It's all some rehearsed bit to pump up the band.

"Tammy? Tammy, are YOU . . . READY?!"

"Yes, ma'am," yells someone else before getting up on stage.

"Are you ready to ride that horse at the head of the team?"

"Yes, ma'am!"

She calls some more girls up there in the same fashion, and they start packing their pretend bags. It seems like some kind of bizarre musical without any music or singing. I'm hoping one of them will burst into song. The whole time Mrs. Busby keeps talking to them. "You better be careful on this trip, June," she says.

"Don't worry about me, ma'am," June says with the utmost confidence. "I know my role!"

"Tammy, are you sure about your horse?"

"Giddyap!" says Tammy and rides a make-believe horse.

The audience laughs and cheers all this stuff. I actually get a laugh, too, when in one part of the bit the girls are tossing the packed bags from girl to girl up to the front girl, but it gets too fast and the front girl ends up getting hit on the head with a bag. She squeals and rubs her head but continues piling the bags up. I'm impressed with her poise.

"We're about to go on a trip, aren't we?" asks Mrs. Busby.

"Yes, ma'am!" say the girls.

"We're about to get on those buses and go to the airport, and where are we going?" Mrs. Busby asks the entire audience.

"New York!" everyone yells. The pep rally's ending by then, and all the students are getting up and getting their gear. I follow the group out into the rain. Most have umbrellas, but some use these red textbooks they all seem to have to cover their heads. I put my backpack over my head as I walk out to the curb where these big black buses have lined up. The band kids are packing their gear into the compartments at the bottom of the buses, where some of the drivers are trying to stuff some white camel suits. They look alive the way their big white hairy heads keep flopping out and those bus drivers are trying to shove them back in. I know they're just suits, but the way those drivers are doing it looks brutal. I mean, if those white camels were really alive, it would be horrible, wouldn't it? Those babies were definitely alive when Daryl shoved them in that bag like potatoes. My hand starts shaking, and I bring down the backpack I've been using to cover myself from the rain, but I'm getting all wet and cold. In the midst of the rain the sun comes out, and for a minute it's raining and sunny at the same time. A superstitious old-timer would have proclaimed the devil must be beating his wife, as the old tale goes. Then the rain stops and the sun keeps shining, but it's all the same to me, constant twilight. I put on my backpack and shove my hands in my pockets. But they won't quit shaking. It feels like my whole body's going to start shaking. Like I'm losing control of myself, and I get scared. I could go to Jim. I can get away just like these band guys going to New York. Escape. When I visited him, I felt a hell of a lot better. Besides, if I took Jim up on his offer, I could spend some time with him, like old times. Yeah. I'd have something to study and girls to look at. And maybe, just maybe, he'll get around to telling me if Mom said anything just before she lost it. I take a deep breath and imagine the devil beating his wife, and the devil looks like Daryl. It's an easy decision. I call Jim and tell him that I'll sit in on his classes but he has to come pick me up right now. He agrees. While I'm waiting I call Dad to tell him I'll be visiting Jim for a few days. He's surprised but glad to hear we'll be spending some time together. I'm glad, too.

CHAPTER 16

JIM SWINGS BY THE SCHOOL IN HIS PICKUP TRUCK and tosses me the keys. "You drive," he says. He turns up the stereo on the classic rock station and stares out the window as I drive home to pick up some clothes. Then we head west. My hands are steady. It's good to be moving, to have a focus, a purpose. Instead of going straight back to Jim's place, he takes me on a short tour of the college, something he's never done. He takes special care to drive me to all the buildings where his classes are. "Don't worry. I'll give you a campus map, clear directions, and my truck. It'll be easy. Here, before I forget." He hands me his student ID card. "This will get you into the gym. It's got everything in there."

"Is there a pool?"

"Yeah, two: one Olympic, one smaller. Don't lose that thing."

"I won't."

"I'll show you the main student parking decks."

We park and walk from the student parking lot to the small downtown area, which is connected to the college. It's almost as if it's an extension of the school. Downtown consists mostly of restaurants, shops, bars, and the like, all set in a half-mile-by-half-mile grid. It makes getting around easy by foot.

"Do you have enough cash?" he asks.

"Yeah."

"While you're here you should try the restaurants, especially when you're at school—just walk up here to town and get something." He walks me around to several inexpensive restaurants of high repute, the highest of them being a Mexican place called Taco Pichu. After having one of their black bean burritos, I know I'll be going back there later in the week. It's massive and costs only three dollars. I didn't think it was possible to fill one's stomach at a restaurant for three dollars, but I was dead wrong and glad of it.

Instead of walking back, we take a campus bus back. It's twice as long as a normal bus and is subdivided into two sections that are connected with this accordion-like center region.

"The bus driver looks young," I say.

"All the campus drivers are students."

"What about the lunchroom ladies?" I'm imagining pretty young lunchroom girls. Then a ton of people get on the bus. All the seats get taken, and so the rest have to stand.

"Incoming freshmen," Jim whispers.

Two girls are standing right beside me. It's so packed in there one of them has to kind of lean over me, and her blond wavy locks hang over my head like vines from a tree. It keeps touching the top of my head. I look up and her face is red. For some reason I feel my spirit lifted a little, my heart beat stronger, and I realize how weak and lost I've felt for the past few weeks. I feel different here. The bus goes onto the campus, where the two girls got off along with everyone else. I can see out the window they're met by a couple of fraternity-looking guys. I find it sad and then annoying. Jim and I get off at the main parking deck. Then it's back to the apartment to relax.

"Here," Jim tosses me a red T-shirt with T-MODEL written across the front.

"Thanks," I say, and put it on over the T-shirt I'm wearing. "Shouldn't it say 'Model-T'?"

"Nope."

I lay out on the sofa watching television while Jim works on his school assignments and readings that have been piling up since he started his job. I don't mind, though. Jim's kind of acting like the old Jim again.

That night I make the mistake of sleeping in Carl's bed again. I dream . . .

. . . I'M WORKING ON A very high-tech offshore oil rig out in the Gulf of Mexico. It looks futuristic, all metal and smooth lines. Almost everything's done by computers and robots. I head a crew of five men who make sure each sector they're in charge of is running smoothly. Then one day the rig is taken over by an evil force. It's those two fleshy masks from Carl's room. They've used their evil to control the machines on the oil rig, which go on a rampage to destroy me and the crew. I lead the crew through a secret small corridor in the heart of the rig. Then through all these glass doors, the last of which is guarded by these gigantic robotic hands that grab one of my men. I dodge the hands and run up to the surface and into the control room where those two masks are. This haunting violin music starts when I see them sitting there on the shelf staring at me with their evil eyes . . .

THEY SCARE ME AWAKE. I take the blankets from Carl's room and crash on the couch. That's the last time I sleep in Carl's bed.

CHAPTER 17

THE NEXT MORNING I GET UP EARLY, have a bowl of cereal, and then put on a pair of Jim's exercise shorts and throw one of his towels in my backpack. I take the truck to the school fitness center, where a security guard who barely even glances at Jim's ID lets me in. Past the running machines and stationary bikes where a dozen or so students are exercising I find the locker room to change. When I get to the swimming area, it's just me and two blonde girls sitting in the corner of the pool talking. One is pretty, and the other isn't so pretty. I get the feeling they've just finished training.

"Are those things allowed in here?" asks the pretty one, pointing at my exercise shorts.

"And isn't he supposed to be wearing a swimming cap?" asks the not-so-pretty one who's attractive regardless.

"Yeah, I think so."

"I don't have a swimming cap," I say.

They both think that's funny.

"If you help me move this table, then we won't say anything this time," says the not-so-pretty attractive one.

I help her move a white plastic table at the end of the smaller pool to a room in the back that's full of chairs and other tables. They go back to sitting in the corner talking, and I start doing laps at my snail's pace. I swim back over to where they are when the not-so-pretty one says, "You look so young. You've gotta be a freshman, right?" She speaks with a little accent, like she's from another country.

"I'm just visiting my brother," I say. "He goes to school here."

"You from Joja, too?" she says with a faux southern accent. It sounds funny coming from a girl with an accent of her own. "I'm from Hawlland."

"You look like real swimmers."

They laugh. "Yah, we are, watch this."

The girl from Holland stands up on the edge and then jumps into the water, wrapping her arms around her folded legs. Her top comes off and she grabs it when she comes up.

"That's not good!" she says.

I want to tell her not to worry because I've seen boobs before, though not in real life, but still, I have seen them. Instead, I get out and jump in, too. Before long I've learned their names are Elise and Heidi, and I'm right, they're both on the swim team. They're both freshmen, and they live in the nearby dorm rooms. They have to leave but before they do, they invite me to stop by sometime, some place called the Ridgeland Girls' Dormitory. Then I have the entire pool to myself for a while. I'm glad because I swim so slowly. It's been a couple years since I've swum. But it's fun, and I feel stronger and better off for it. Not only because of the swimming but those girls were nice, too. Daryl seems a millions miles away at that moment. With girls like these around I feel safe from the likes of him. Not that they could beat him up or anything, but he wouldn't come into a place like this. He wouldn't belong there. I keep doing my laps until a middle-aged woman and an old lady show up. Then I head out.

Jim doesn't get up until late in the afternoon. He gets a bowl of cereal and tosses me a psychology textbook. "This is for Monday."

"What? I have to read this by Monday?" I lie back on the sofa and peruse the pages.

"Just chapter seventeen," he says. "That class is big, but we do a lot of group work, and she's always giving pop quizzes on the previous chapter. Otherwise, I could just skip class and get the notes from my buddies. I already told Mitch and Chang you'd be there for me. So just hook up with them. Mitch's a short-haired Jewish guy. You know Chang."

"Sure."

"I can take care of school and work tomorrow myself, but I'm gonna need the truck to get around, so how about I give you a ride to campus in the afternoon? I'll finish work and stop by before I go to school, that way you can sleep in and then hang out on campus."

Jim gets on his computer and starts working on an English paper while I try to read the chapter in the psychology textbook. Not only is it complicated as hell, but because I haven't read the rest of the book, I keep having to go back and look things up. I only get through half of it before I get irritated and turn to the television, which is showing a documentary on a rock star from the seventies who had everything and then lost it all. There's even a reenactment of when he gets fired by his band, beginning with a close-up shot of his face when he says, "You insult me and now you kick me out of the band? You 'bleep bleep bleep' looking down on me, you 'bleep.'" Then the camera pans away, and you can hear him vomiting. The camera turns back and shows him promptly throwing up all over the floor. There's a deliberate out-of-focus shot of the vomit discoloring the floor. I turn to the Food Channel.

CHAPTER 18

AN OFFICE BUDDY PICKS JIM UP FOR WORK early Monday morning. I stay on the sofa with my eyes closed until he's gone, then have a bowl of cereal before going back to sleep. It isn't until ten AM that I get up for my first day of college. I throw on my jeans and T-shirt and head out.

After parking in the main deck I follow the map to the psychology building. I feel like a real college student trying to find my class on the first day of school. In high school the new kid always immediately gets talked about and sized up. Not here. That's what's so great about it. All these other college students don't know who I am, and they don't give a rat's ass. I ask around and finally find the lecture hall. It's almost like a big fancy movie theater in there, except all the seats have small foldout desktops. There's a uniformed guard at a desk checking IDs, just like at the gym. Once I step in, I realize I'm not even sure exactly what a Jew's supposed to look like and I can't find Chang in among the seats. I figure if Mitch and Chang see some guy looking around, they'll guess it's me, so I stand at the front looking around. Sure enough a couple of guys in the back wave. I go up the carpeted stairs where they've saved me a seat. Chang introduces me to Mitch. It's no wonder I couldn't recognize Chang, what with his long hair hanging down his back instead of tied in a ponytail like I remember it. Mitch, well, Mitch wears this stocking cap over what looks like short brown hair. If that's what a Jew looks like, then that's fine by me.

An older lady wearing a gray business suit comes in, and everyone gets quiet. It turns out to be true that teachers teach, and professors profess. She gets up there and starts talking off the top of her head about numerous topics that weren't covered in the chapter I read. She even brings up Jane Park, a famous psychologist and novelist I've read up on. She mentions the idea of the subconscious and how it can bubble up in the forms of feelings and ideas that may seem unlike the person. Inversely, one can also go into the subconscious through various means, including therapy, meditation, or psychoactive drugs. She goes and riffs on a number of topics: primacy and action, sexuality as initiation. She keeps talking, and I keep taking notes like everyone else. Then about halfway through class she tells us to get in our groups and write a short essay about how the id, ego, and superego relate to Jane Park's ideas of "character repugnance" and "character acceptance." We can go at it in any way we want, she says. "Remember," she adds, "this is going to be scaled." Then she lets us loose for the rest of the class to write the essay.

"What does scaled mean?" I ask.

"It means all the scores are relative to each other. If everyone gets fifty and you get a sixty, you get an A. If everyone gets ninety-nine and you get a ninety, you get an F. So what that means is we're competing with everyone," Chang explains.

"Got it."

"Did you get what she's lecturing about?" asks Mitch.

"Yeah, I read some Jane Park at the school library."

"You mean not in this textbook?"

"Yeah, I read *The Energy Exchange: People Relating to People and Yourself*. That was cool because she told these dark fairy tales to illustrate her points about transference of the inner world to the outer."

"Dude, don't talk so loud," Mitch whispers. "We've hit the bonanza."

"Some people think she's a little weird," I say. "But she's a leading social psychologist."

"Damn, man, let's write this thing."

We huddle up and write an essay that brings together most of the main ideas that I remember from her books. It's kind of beyond the lecture, but it still contains the main points the professor seemed to be emphasizing. The question's so open-ended, I'm really not sure what the professor wants. Mitch assures me we'll ace it.

After we're finished Chang leaves for another class, and Mitch and I walk across campus into town, where loud music's blaring out from the square. There's a banner up across the thoroughfare for the Saint Ignatius Church of Wonderment. An aging country rock singer wearing a Hawaiian shirt is up on a stage set against the steps of city hall. He takes a sip out of a red plastic cup and then gets on the microphone and says, "If you people had to pay for this, you'd have already paid a thousand dollars each!" Then he starts into a country song about the oceans of love in a girl's heart out in the universe somewhere.

I get a Coke from a vending machine and sit down with Mitch at one of the many outdoor tables. "So, you wanna toke it up?" Mitch asks.

"What?" I ask.

"Go smoke some weed."

"Ah, right. Sorry, I gotta take the truck back to Jim. He says he needs it."

"Right. Carl."

"What about Carl?" I ask.

"Jim's always doing favors for him. Things like writing papers, picking up food for him, all kinds of crap."

"You're saying that's why he needs the truck today?"

"Chang told me he thinks Jim's helping one of Carl's friends move."

"What's wrong with that?"

"He thinks Carl's his friend." Mitch gets up and puts on his backpack. "Maybe he is. I don't know. Have you met Carl?"

"Not yet."

"Decide for yourself."

I sit there awhile after Mitch leaves, wondering what the hell's going on with Jim. I don't know what to believe, but whatever it is, it doesn't sound good. I go back to the parking deck and drive over to the office Jim gave me directions to. He's waiting for me at the front. "How was class?" he asks me.

"Good. We did a writing assignment, and I already knew the topic. Mitch and Chang seemed pretty sure we'd get an A. I mean you'd get an A."

"Easy, right?" he says. I'm wanting to ask him about what Mitch said, but I can't do it. I'm worried it's true, and I don't want to embarrass him. I can't ever remember feeling that way about Jim. It doesn't seem right that a younger brother should do that to his older brother. So I keep my trap shut. He drives me back to the apartment before taking off. I try to distract myself with some daytime television, but there's nothing on and I keep thinking about what Mitch said. I decide to go on an expedition. First thing I do is get on Jim's laptop and check the Web site for the anime expo I had seen advertised in that bar when Jason and Chang were there. Of all the things Yoshi could have missed—friends, family, or even food—it was anime he mentioned that day we busted out of lockdown. I want to see what the hell that's all about. It's all happening at a major mall across town, the kind with a big movie complex, so I check the local bus routes and find a connector on Leland Street three blocks up. I leave Jim a note telling him I'm going to the expo and then walk down to the bus stop. With two transfers, it's almost an hour to get there, but I get there.

The entire mall is crawling with nerds, tons of them. A lot of them are dressed up in crazy outfits: sailor girls, robots, trolls, elves, and little monsters abound. Not all of them are nerds, though. There're some punks, jocks, and even some good-looking girls, too. But they're all really excited and having a blast. Those deformed babies would fit right in, I think. I pick up a flier and find a listing of anime movies showing. I decide on *Vampire Incarnation*. The movie is about a city of vampires where humans are used as cattle for their blood. But a group of humans revolt and fight back. The problem is, the only way they can fight the vampires is to become vampires themselves. It's got to be one of the most violent movies I've ever seen in my life. The small group of once-human vampires essentially has to kill every vampire in that city, and they do it in the goriest of ways. Because it's a cartoon they show everything: body parts fly off, explode, melt, get eaten. When it's over, I walk out of the theater actually needing a drink to calm my nerves. There's a restaurant right across from the theater, so I get a table and just order a Coke. The interior of the place is all red and full of anime fans. I'm too chicken to order a beer. I got to remember to get a fake ID. Across from me is a pretty lady in a red dress drinking with two nerds. They're drinking some red liquid in blue glasses. I keep staring at them, and eventually the lady smiles and pushes a glass to the corner of their table as an invitation. *Hot damn*, I think. I go sit down with her two nerd minions.

"Hello," the lady says.

"Hi," I say back.

"Have a drink," she says.

"All right." I take a sip. "Is this wine?" I ask.

"No, it's called blood sangria."

"Blood?"

"There's no real blood in there."

I take another sip, and one of the nerds says, "You don't drink it like that," and he starts chugging his glass. The other nerds start chanting, "Chug, chug, chug!" Some of the other tables join in. "Chug, chug, chug!"

I realize then that the lady's red dress resembles one of the characters in *Vampire Incarnation*. Others in the restaurant are dressed as some of the characters. The nerd can't finish and ends up spitting some up on his white shirt. It really does look like blood. Some guys from the other tables dressed as vampires come to help him as he looks like he's going to pass out. Then I start chugging. Everyone starts in again, "Chug, chug, chug!" Even the guys helping the drunken fellow stop and chant. I don't think I can do it. But halfway through my glass it feels like I'm not even drinking, like I have my mouth open and it's just going down. Everyone cheers and my cup is refilled. I do it one more time, and then my mind officially becomes muddied with blood sangria. It's so damn sweet, it starts making me feel sick. That's when Jim shows up out of nowhere looking for me.

"There you are!" he says.

"I'm drinking blood sangria!"

"C'mon, let's get out of here."

I thank the lady and her remaining sober nerd minion before leaving. I follow Jim out with blood sangria coursing through my veins. "I can't believe you took the bus. No one takes the bus," he says.

"Old people do," I say. "And Mexicans. And me."

We're walking through the corridors of the mall when Jim confesses, "I need a drink."

"You, too?" I ask.

"One for the road. I had a long day at work." I notice that he's not wearing the dress shirt and pants that he had on when I picked him up for work. He's got on jeans and a T-shirt, clothes much more appropriate for moving things.

We stop by a little tavern close to the entrance of the mall, where the people look normal, more like yuppies and students. "Where are the nerds?" I ask. The people at the bar start laughing. They seem like older yuppie types.

"You've reached the green zone," someone says.

"The nerds and freaks stay in that section over there! We stay on this side."

"I didn't mean it like that," I say. "They're okay. They have a right to be whatever they are. They're humans like us. Flesh and blood," I add. They think that's even funnier. The bartender, a pretty young blonde, checks Jim's ID. I tell her, "I'm not drinking. Just water please. I'm full of blood sangria."

"Whoa," she says. "I'm impressed."

I think she's being sarcastic, but I can't tell. I'm too drunk. Jim orders a beer and that's when I ask, "How come Chang and Jason don't like Carl?"

"Carl's kind of abrasive. But he has a good heart."

"But none of your friends seem to like him."

"They just don't know him. If they got to know him, they'd like him."

I nod and drink my water, but he's starting to make me sad. After he finishes his beer we go back to his apartment, where I hit the sofa.

CHAPTER 19

THE NEXT DAY JIM COMES BY AND PICKS ME UP from the apartment early in the afternoon. It's a nice sunny day, so I'm glad to get out. From the campus parking deck he goes to his class and I walk around campus. There're hordes of students walking about, or sitting or lying around. It seems so leisurely and quiet, nothing like the chaos of high school. And the girls, there're so many pretty girls. Just being around them puts me in a good mood. So I sit down on the lawn in front of the library like so many of the other students and watch the people go by for most of the afternoon.

When it gets later, I take a stroll to the western edge of campus where there's a small two-level mall. I go in to have a look around. A bunch of high-school punks with spiked hair and Mohawks wearing tuxedos and dresses are coming down the escalator by the fountain. Behind them come a gaggle of people dressed in strange getups, ranging from vampires to robots. The anime heads are apparently every-where. *Good,* I think, *the more variety the better.* Hell, if I had an outfit of my own I'd join them. After I stuff myself with a couple steak bur-ritos, I walk around until I find the rear exit that goes out into a big parking lot. I don't feel like backtracking all the way through the mall and through the school so instead walk out to the road. At the first intersection I see that the road I'm on is the road Jim's apartment is on, Leland Street. With the fuel of the steak burritos in me I figure, I can walk it. Along the way this froggish-looking guy comes along with me. He catches up to me and says, "Did you see that? Those guys dressed up in there?" He's just a student by the looks of it. He has a backpack and nice clothes on. It's just that his face looks kind of froglike.

"Yeah," I say.

"Where you going?" he asks me.

"Home, I just decided to walk."

"Me, I gotta walk to work after school. Usually I get a ride or catch a bus, but I gotta walk it today. Hey, watch this," he says, and runs up ahead of me. A black Lexus is pulling out from a side road, and he throws himself against it. It looks real, like maybe it hit him hard, but I can tell it's just a glancing blow. A girl jumps out of the car screaming.

"Oh my God!" she yells.

"Jesus," I say. I pull out my cell phone to call Jim.

"Wait! Wait! Who are you calling?" she says.

"My brother, to come pick my ass up! I'm through with walking! I'm tired!"

"Wait, I'll take you and your friend wherever you want to go!"

"He's not my friend," I say.

"Come on," says the frog-looking student. "Come on. I did all that work."

"Just up the road, okay?" I say. Froggy fake hobbles into the car and nudges me. "Man, you're nuts," I say. The girl drops me off and then says she'd take "my friend" wherever he needs to go. "He's not my friend," I say before slamming the door. I carefully ascend the steps up to the apartment. The door's already open.

"Heeeeyyyy!" says Naomi as she gets up from the sofa and gives me a hug. She smells like alcohol and a very nice-smelling perfume.

"What are you doing here?" I look around for Carl or Jim.

"I was waiting for you. Carl told me you're visiting Jim. Why didn't you call me?"

"I . . . sorry, I don't even know your number."

"I didn't give that to you? Huh. Oh well. Let's go," she takes my hand and pulls me out.

"Where're we going?"

"I'm hungry."

We walk down the steps. "You remember at the wedding pictures you told me you were the smart one?" she asks.

"Sure."

"Do you think I'm one of the smart ones?"

"That's like asking a pretty person if they're pretty, right?"

She smiles and says, "Maybe."

"How badly do you want to be smart?" I say kind of suggestively, which surprises me in a good way. She laughs and puts her arm around my shoulder and with her other hand guides my arm around her waist. Even though it's summer, there's a chill in the air. I'm wearing my light black hoodie, which I take off. "Take it," I insist. She's wearing a sleeveless black thing. "Take it." And she does. One of those big college buses goes *vroom*ing by.

"Have you ridden one of those?" she asks me.

"Once."

"Me, too. One time. There's one that goes to the airport. I took it when I went down and saw you. Here, you're driving." She tosses me the keys to her older-model BMW, and we're off to downtown. I follow the procedure, cruise around until a spot appears, then slip in like a thief. She smiles admiringly at me. "Now that's what I like: a guy in control of the situation." If only she knew how wrong she was.

When we're getting out of the car, a girl's voice yells, "Hey, boy! So that's why you didn't visit!" It was the pretty girl from the swimming pool walking the other way across the street. "Not bad!" she says.

"Who was that?" asks Naomi.

"She's a swimmer."

"A swimmer, huh? Come on, you man about town."

Naomi takes me to a diner, where I have the meat loaf. She gets one, too. I can't get myself to tell her I'm full of steak burrito, so I stuff down the meat loaf like a man's man. It's torture. I think I'm going to die, but I manage to eat most of it.

"I think I ate too much," I say.

"I got something for that."

"What is it?"

"You'll see."

She pays for the check and drives us to a Motel 6 close by. She explains Carl's going to show up at her place at some point tonight and she's not in the mood for his "idiocy," as she calls it.

"Is he always like that?"

"No, in fact, he used to never be like that. But he's different now. Wait here, I'll get the room."

I stand outside the car until she comes back and takes me to a room on the third floor. "I'm gonna take a shower. You need to use it?"

"No, go ahead. Hey, about that thing for overeating?"

"After my shower."

I sit at the edge of the bed and flip through the channels, not really watching. *Good God, what's she going to do?* I wonder. No. No chance of that happening. She doesn't hardly even know me. Look at me. Skinny sixteen-year-old kid. But why would she bring me here? No, she just wants to get away from Carl, that's all. Don't even think like that. Isn't that the way sleazeballs think? I mean, consider Carl. He doesn't— My train of thought is shattered when she comes out in her panties and camisole with a towel wrapped around her wet hair. She walks over to her purse and pulls out a little bag.

"What's that?" I ask.

"You wanna know why you shouldn't touch little bags like this?"

"Why?"

"Because that's where people keep their change ... or their weed."

She comes back to bed holding a marijuana joint, which she lights with a small orange lighter and puffs on with a furrowed brow. I look over on my bed stand, where an ashtray is, and put it on her exposed white thigh. She gives me the joint and then dries her hair some more. I inhale on the moistened paper, and fire and ash shoot down my throat into my lungs. I cough and hand the joint back to Naomi, who tosses the towel onto the floor.

"Are you okay?" she asks, rubbing my back.

I nod my head and say, "Yes," in between a cough. By the time my coughing dies down she's already smoked some more and is handing it back to me. I take smaller puffs and I'm okay. The third time it comes around I take too much into my lungs again and cough so hard I think I'll vomit.

"I'll get you some water," she says. I grab her arm and shake my head. I get up out of the bed and walk slowly to the bathroom, though it seems I'm moving very fast. My head is swirling. The mirror's still steamed up, but I can see my blurry face. My eyes don't look like my eyes. They're red and animal-like. I look like a beast just come out of a primeval forest.

"What's goin' on in there?" she asks.

"I'm looking at myself in the mirror, but it doesn't look like me."

"Who does it look like?"

"A Neanderthal man ..." I say. Then I whisper, "... of the hunter-gatherer persuasion."

Who is this guy? I think, looking into the mirror. My hair's gotten a little longish. Kind of shaggy. I look like a beast. I wipe my wet mouth, then go back into the room, which is thick with marijuana smoke. I bet the inside of my lungs look like that. Naomi's sitting there with her back against the headrest with her legs sprawled out. She puts out the joint and sits back with a groan. She puts her arms out and says, "Come here, Samuel."

I crawl into bed, and she takes me into her arms and holds me tight. Holding each other like that, I forget about that beastly face, my stuffed belly, almost like a pregnant woman. She starts kissing me and I kiss back. Her breath smells like wine. She puts her hands into my pants and rubs me. It seems so quiet in the room, as if the entire world had stopped and the only thing that could be heard is our breathing.

"Is this okay?" she asks me.

I say, "Yes." I'm so scared it's crazy.

She reaches for her little bag and pulls out a condom.

"I thought that was for change and weed."

"And condoms." She smiles. "You want me to?"

"I got it," I say. I'd never put one on and now regret not practicing, but I know how from a book I read once. It's different in real life, though, and I'm not sure if I'm not doing it inside out. Naomi takes it and places it on me. Without a word she gets on top of me. I feel like I'm melting into her, disappearing into perfect warmth. Cold doesn't exist in this place. She starts moving and the fire below becomes a sun, and then a supernova, and then the big bang, and then I'm done, just like that.

"Sorry," I say.

"That's okay," she lies down on top of me. I can't believe it just happened. It's unbelievable. My body tingles and my heart races. I feel stronger. Energized. She moves to the side of me and holds me. I get up to use the bathroom, and when I do I see myself in the mirror again. I do look like a beast, wild hair, naked, just had sex. I can't help but smile. I can imagine myself with a beard and a mullet . . . and a blue cap. The thought of it doesn't scare me at all. I continue smiling all the way back to the bed, where Naomi is dozing. For now it's good to lie down with Naomi, but I feel like I could run a marathon and then climb a mountain afterward.

NAOMI DROPS ME OFF AT JIM'S in the morning before going off to her classes. No one's there, so I lie on the couch watching television most of the morning. My head feels like that swamp back in Sugweepo, all muddy and thick. I doze off a few times, and then in the late morning Carl shows up. He's in running pants and a sleeveless T-shirt, and there's a silver chain around his neck. I get up, seeing as how it is his place. The guy stands a foot above me. "'Sup, dude," he says, and sticks out his hand.

I've gotten up and say, "What's up?" Then when he grips my hand, he grips it real hard and looks at my face for a reaction. It's just like Daryl all over again except his grip isn't as strong. I'm able to keep a straight face but the diamond ring he's wearing pinches my skin. He finally lets go.

"So you're Jim's brother, huh?" He looks me up and down, and I already don't like him.

"Yeah, I'm Jim's brother."

"Speak up."

"Yeah, I'm Jim's brother."

"Jim says you didn't come back here last night." I just glare back at him. "Well?" He sits down on the couch. "What'd you do?"

"I stayed at a friend's."

"What friend do you have here?"

"A girl I met at the pool. She's on the swim team. Her name is Heidi. She's from Holland. She stays in the Ridgeland Girls' Dormitory. Satisfied?"

He stares at me for a while and smiles. "You just saved your ass from a world of pain." He heads out the door, but before leaving he turns and says derisively, "I can't believe your Jim's brother." He's big and ugly but doesn't scare me. I don't like him at all, but he doesn't scare me.

When Jim gets home, the two of us cook ramen noodles for dinner. I don't mention Carl. I might hate the guy, but he's still Jim's friend, and I didn't come up and visit Jim after such a long time of distance and silence to mess up his life. Instead, I catch him up on Dad: older and grayer but the same ole dad, Trixi the cat's comings and goings, some of my adventures at school—what with detention and my video project and the field party debacle. He has some good laughs. It's more of the old Jim. I just hope he stays this way.

"I wish my life was as exciting as yours. Me, I just work, go to classes, and study. I mean, I go out and drink with my buddies some-times, but that's about it. Why, you've had more luck with the girls than I've had for a while."

"Normal's good. I'd take normal any day over craziness."

"Yeah, maybe you're right. I have more fun than I let on. It's just when I'm not having fun, I'm pretty busy. Always busy. "

"Remember what Mom says, appreciate what you have, and you'll get what you need."

"Right. Hey, let's play some PlayStation football."

"You don't have work?"

"I'll do it later, come on."

THAT NIGHT WHILE I'M SLEEPING on the couch my dream continues . . .

. . . I'M WORKING ON A very high-tech offshore oil rig out in the Gulf
of Mexico. It looks futuristic, all metal and smooth lines. Almost everything's done by computers and robots. I head a crew of five men
who make sure each sector they're in charge of is running smoothly.
Then one day the rig is taken over by an evil force. It's those two
fleshy masks from Carl's room. They've used their evil to control the
machines on the oil rig, which go on a rampage to destroy the crew
and me. I lead the crew through a secret small corridor in the heart
of the oil rig. Then through all these glass doors, the last of which is
guarded by these gigantic robotic hands that grab one of my men. I
dodge the hands and run up to the surface and into the control room,
where those two masks are. This haunting violin music starts when I
see them sitting there on the shelf. The masks turn into the faces of
Daryl and Carl. They scare me more in my dream than in real life.
Then I realize the one on the right has no power. It's that one on the
left. So I grab it with a piece of paper because I don't want to touch it
with my hand, and throw it against the wall. Then I stomp on it. I free
my men and we escape on a helicopter that takes us to my house in
Sugweepo. In the backyard of my house there's a much bigger, newly
built house with a nice picket fence around it. I suddenly remember
I've a seed in my pocket, and it's very important. I announce to the
crew and my dad and Jim that I have the seed. They all want me to
plant it, but I don't want to do it in front of them. It embarrasses me,

so I kind of just toss it out onto the ground, feeling it will grow just fine on its own. No one sees it, but it's glowing white. I see that it's glowing from the porch light of the new house shining on it. I tell everyone how we have to do this for my mom before entering the new house. And up in the window of the house, above the porch light, I see my mom looking down on me with this big smile on her face, and she's saying something to me but I can't hear her. "What? I can't hear you?" I say.

Then my mother begins to open the window . . .

CHAPTER 20

T HE NEXT DAY JIM WAKES ME UP EARLY before his ride picks
him up for work. He gives me the English literature paper he's
been working on and tells me to submit it when I get to class.
"There's going to be a special speaker, so just take notes," he tells me.
"If anyone gives you a problem, just tell them I'm sick and you're
there to help out. Don't forget to hand that paper in."

I leave early to make sure I can find the classroom. Jim's directions are good, and I get there in plenty of time. There's no ID check,
and the classroom looks like a small conference room. There's one big
long table with students all around it. I get a seat and try to look like
I'm supposed to be there. I take out Jim's paper and pretend to read
it. Everyone gets quiet when a lady in a charcoal gray suit and short
blond hair finally shows up with another older lady. I hand in Jim's
paper with everyone else.

"Are you in the right class?" she asks me.

"I'm here for Jim Polk."

"You look a little young to be in college," she says.

"I'm his brother. I'm still in high school."

"If only we all had little brothers like you. Now I'm going to have to ask you to leave. Only enrolled students are allowed in this class. Nothing personal."

"Will you take the paper?"

"Yes, I'll take the paper. Maybe I'll see you in a few years, young man."

I walk back to the parking deck and take Jim's truck for a drive around town. I take out one of the cigarettes from the pack Jason had given me and manage to smoke it without coughing my lungs out. It makes me a little nauseous, but it also gives me a serious buzz that cheers me up. After my leisure drive I go back to the apartment. Carl and Naomi are sitting on the couch.

"Hey!" Naomi says, and gets up to give me a friendly but distant hug. "Long time no see!" She gives me a sly wink before letting go. I try not to smile too hard.

"Ah yes," I say, "that wedding rehearsal."

Jim comes out of the kitchen wearing an apron and oven mitts. "What happened?" he says. "Did you go to class?"

"Yeah, and I gave her the paper then she kicked me out."

"Kicked you out of class?"

"She said no one's allowed to sit in for students, but she wasn't angry or anything. She invited me back when I'm older."

"But she did take the paper?"

"Yeah, she said she was cool with that. What about you? I thought you had to work."

"Oh, I went in and they said they didn't need me. Sorry, bro, if I would have known . . ."

"Don't worry about it."

"You know Naomi," Jim says.

"Yeah, sure," I say. "How've you been?"

"Good. And you?"

"Okay."

"Yeah?"

"Yeah."

"Wassup, dude," Carl says from the couch.

I nod.

"That's Carl," says Jim.

"Samuel's the one who drove two hours—" says Naomi.

"I know I know. You've told me already about a thousand times."

"I can't believe you came up!" Naomi says, and gives me another hug.

"Me, neither."

"How the hell did you get up here anyhow? Aren't you too young to be driving this far on your own?" says Carl.

"He's smarter than you," says Jim, poking his head out of the kitchen. I can smell some cooking going on in there.

"Hardy har har! You must have saved a lot of milk money."

"Carl, why are you doing this?" asks Naomi.

"I'm just kidding," he says.

"I do have some money. Angie paid me to come to the rehearsal, and then I sold some old comic books a few weeks ago that gave me even more."

"Comic books?" says Carl. His eyes light up. "How do you expect to get a woman reading comic books?"

"Shut up, Carl," says Naomi.

"I'm serious. You'll stay a virgin the rest of your life. At best you might get an ugly heifer. A real woman wouldn't take some weak comic-book faggot. Well, maybe a weak comic-book heifer."

"Don't listen to Carl. He can be a jerk sometimes."

The thing is, I think he might be right. Suddenly I feel weak and cowardly. Like when I'm around Daryl. My face begins to get hot, and I'm sure it's red. I hold back the urge to tell him about Naomi and me. "It's okay," I say. I get up and walk to the doorway. Jim might be in the kitchen, but I know he could hear everything. I feel like I should go somewhere else, somewhere far away and where maybe I can find my courage. But I don't know where to go. This was the last place I knew.

Jim comes out with these burritos covered in some kind of peanut sauce that he's heated up. He puts the plates on the table for him and Carl. The shame and cowardice I feel turns to rage. I want to punch Carl in the face, but I know I won't do it. I go into the bathroom on the verge of tears. I can't bear to look at myself in the mirror, so I turn quickly to the window and punch it out. It shatters, and I hear a scream. Naomi comes running in. I look up at Naomi and then down at my bloody hand.

"Oh my God! Samuel, what'd you do?" She wraps a towel around my hand. While she's doing that I see my face in the mirror. It's the one I saw when I was with Naomi. The primal man. I feel better, stronger, and it's like that strength is coming back to me. She pulls me out of the bathroom. Carl and my brother are standing behind the coffee table.

"Did he break something?" says Carl.

"What happened?" asks Jim.

"We're going to the hospital," says Naomi. Carl walks over and grabs Naomi.

"Why are you doing this?" he says.

"I'm not doing anything! Samuel needs to go to the hospital. So get your hands off of me!"

She jerks her arm away, but he won't let loose. He stares at her like he wants to hit her. Naomi jerks her arm again, and he lets go this time. As I walk by, Carl says, "Go home to Momma, pussy," and I swing my bloody hand, landing my forearm against the front of his throat just like Daryl did to me that night in the house. Carl's face goes red and he starts choking. I swing a roundhouse left, missing him the first time, but I keep throwing that left until I hit him on his right temple and he crumples. I can feel the power. Not only the power of violence and action but the power of standing up to evil. Jim and Naomi just stare in shock as I take the plate of burritos and smash it on his head.

"Samuel, stop!" Naomi grabs a hold of me while Jim looks on, disbelievingly.

I stomp on his ribs a couple of times. Naomi tries to push me back. I look Jim square in the eye and point down at Carl, "Friend or no friend, you're wrong. He doesn't have a good heart." Naomi drags me away, down the stairs to her car.

"Why'd you do that?" she asks.

"He had it coming to him," I say. She turns out onto the road and starts speeding toward school. "Why are you even with him?" I say angrily. "He's a dirtbag."

After a long silence, she says, "I don't know."

"Maybe you deserve each other."

She starts to cry, and I feel like a complete heel. I hope she kicks me out of the car or at least turns around, but she goes all the way to the emergency wing of the college hospital and even comes with me. I let her. In the waiting room is a lady with her kid and an old couple along with a random assortment of people. There's lots of coughing going on. A chubby middle-aged nurse at the front desk asks, "So what happened to your hand, Rocky?"

"I punched out a window." Right after I say it, I wonder if I should have lied. Maybe it's illegal to punch out windows.

"A window?" she turns to Naomi. "What about you? Are you all right?"

"I'm fine, I'm fine. It's him who's hurt," Naomi says, her eyes puffy and red.

"Well, punching a window's original. Now why would you want to do that, honey?" asks the nurse.

"I got angry," I say.

"Now what would your mother say about that?"

"My mother died a year ago," I say. My hand had been feeling numb and tingly up till then, but a hot wave of pain starts to cover it. It makes me want to cry, but I hold back.

"Honey, I'm sorry to hear that," says the nurse.

"I'm over it." But I feel like a bastard for saying it.

"Let me take a look at that." She peels open the towel. "Ooh, that is nasty. Just for that you get put at the top of the waiting list!" She folds the towel back up. "You're lucky your girlfriend here was nice enough to bring you here. Come on. Follow me."

"I was wondering if this could go under my name. He's not a student here, but I am," says Naomi.

The nurse looks at the form again. "Sixteen years old! Talk about cradle robbing! Ha!"

"I'm just a family friend," says Naomi.

"I'll talk to the doctor about it. Come on."

We walk down a corridor full of gurneys when right in front of us three big male nurses dressed in white gang tackle some man who was trying to get away.

"Get off me, you apes!" he yells. "Get off me, ahhhh!"

"My, my, you chose a busy night to visit us," says the nurse.

We follow her to a smaller room, where she pulls back some

drapes around a bed. "Wait here." I sit down on the bed, and we wait without speaking to each other. The doctor shows up after a while. He's a serious-looking young black man. "Says here you punched a window, is that right?"

"Yes, sir."

"Whatever you punched and wherever you were, were police involved?"

"No sir, it was at my brother's apartment. I just got angry."

"It's true, I was there," attests Naomi. "It was kind of my fault. My boyfriend was being a jerk."

"So you're saying I don't have to fill out a report on this, right?"

"Yes, he just punched out a window."

"Good, because I hate filling out those reports." He smiles. "Let me take a look," he says. "Hmm . . ." He has a nurse clean the wound and then he puts in five stitches across my first three fingers. Then they wrap it up before leaving Naomi and me there.

"Does it hurt?" Naomi asks without looking at me.

"It's okay, just throbbing a little," I say. "I'm sorry about what I said."

She continues looking away without a word. I lie back in the bed, and I'm reminded of my mom. She was lying in a bed just like this. Jim comes through the drapes and looks at me wide-eyed. "Are you okay?" he asks. "Why are you lying down like that?"

"Reminds you of Mom, doesn't it?"

He just looks at me, kind of shocked. "I'm sorry, Samuel, I should've done something about that guy. I thought I owed him something, but I don't owe him anything. That's not friendship. You're right. Everyone was right. He's a complete asshole, and I'll kick his ass for you one time myself. I promise."

"What'd Mom say before she lost her mind?" I ask.

"What?"

"She had to have said something. You were the last one. You."

Jim takes a deep breath and pinches his brow. "She wasn't making any sense, Samuel. The tumor had metastasized all over by then. She was already deep in dementia."

"I don't care. What did she say?"

"She said, 'The weather's turning . . . don't forget your coat . . . listen . . . listen . . . this darkness . . . it's getting dark . . .' See it doesn't make any sense. 'Don't forget your coat'? It's just random memories. It's all random."

"I don't care if it's random. What else? Tell me, Jim."

"Uh, what else she said, 'When I get to where I'm going, I'll call to let you know I'm okay . . . I'll give you a call . . . it's getting dark . . . but it's not yours . . . listen closely . . . I'll call . . . it's getting so dark, son, I better leave the light on . . . I'll leave the light on for you, son.'"

It makes me think of the dream I'd been having, the one on the oil rig and the evil masks. When my mom opens the window, she's going to say, 'I'll leave the light on for you, son.' That's what she'd say when it was getting late. When it was twilight. I take out my wallet and in the folds behind my driver's license I take out the picture of my mom. It's not there. She's gone. *That's right. That's right. I forgot that bastard took it.* "Goddamnit!"

"What is it?" asks Naomi.

In its place is a torn Polaroid picture of me, lying unconscious by the bed with those babies lying by my head. It wasn't lightning. It was the flash of a camera. Daryl. He'd taken a picture of me when I was lying unconscious. "I'm gonna kill him," I say.

"What?" Jim and Naomi ask in unison.

"Kill who?" asks Jim.

"Just a figure of speech," I say, trying to appear calm. "I need to go home."

"You mean now?" Jim asks.

"Yeah, right now."

"Why?"

I'm up and moving. "Naomi, you think you could take me home."

"I guess so," she says.

"Samuel. Samuel. I'll take you, okay?" says Jim. "If you want to go, we'll go. Come on."

"I gotta go," I tell Naomi.

"Are you sure everything's okay?"

"Yeah. I just need to get home." I try to lighten the mood by saying, "I got issues."

She chuckles at that. "Don't we all. Carl really is a creep, isn't he?"

"I hope you get the strength . . . no . . . the self-respect to dump him," I say. She gives me a hug, and I'm reminded of all I've experienced the past few days, all that my body has experienced. And I keep thinking about it in the truck as Jim drives us back to Sugweepo: the dreams, the college classes, the girls at the pool, on the bus, Naomi, the marijuana, Jason telling me how to win a fight, to never stop fighting—all of it. So much in so little time. It now feels like I'm wearing new flesh, and I feel somehow more natural and stronger. Even the little things like the anime expo stand out. That movie about the vampires seems so vivid. To pass the time in the truck I tell Jim about that anime movie and how in order to defeat the vampires the hero had to become one.

"I'll have to check that out," he says. "If you can get that Tempo working, maybe you can come back and catch the last part of that expo."

"That's a good idea. I could bring Yoshi."

"Who's Yoshi?"

"A Japanese exchange student. He loves anime."

"Thanks," he says.

"For what?"

"For showing me something I couldn't see. I can't believe I was friends with that guy. What was I thinking?"

"Don't worry. He was probably all sneaky about it."

"Very sneaky." He nods. "Jason's going to officially become your best friend when he finds out what you did. All my buddies will."

I check my watch, and it's already five. The sun is beginning to turn amber. What I need to do needs to be done before it gets too dark. Twilight should be fine. Just enough light.

WHEN WE GET HOME, JIM HEADS FOR THE KITCHEN, asking, "When's Dad get home?"

"I'm not sure," I say, and go straight to my room and grab that knife out from under my pillow. I go into the kitchen to find Jim's getting some sandwich meat out of the fridge. "Can I borrow your truck?" I ask.

"How long are you going to be?"

"Not long."

"You think you can drive a stick with that hand?"

"It shouldn't be a problem."

I take the keys and go out to the truck. It jerks and stalls, and I end up accidentally honking the horn. "Shit," I whisper. I don't have time for this. I've got to get to those babies. I pull onto the front lawn and drive onto the road from there. Shifting the gears with my bum hand stings a little, but isn't that bad. I drive straight to Mrs. Greenan's house, hoping they'll be there. The neighborhood is still its quiet, desolate self. The Charger isn't there, but I'm still tensed up and ready with the knife. I take a deep breath and get out. I hurry to the door and bang on it. "Mrs. Greenan! Mrs. Greenan!" I hear quick shuffling steps and the door opens.

"Samuel!"

"Where are they?"

"Daryl. Daryl took them somewheres."

"Where'd he take them?"

"I don't know. It was my fault. God. God told me he was doing terrible things to my babies. I didn't believe him . . . but then I—"

"Have you checked his hunting shed?"

"Shed?"

"The one in the woods back behind the Kmart."

"No."

"I'm gonna get them. You just wait here," I say.

I run out to the truck and, after a few jerks and one stall out, get driving as fast as she'll take me out to the Kmart. There's a steady stream of shoppers pushing their red shopping carts out of the store. They remind me to calm down and drive slowly, even though my mind is going a thousand miles per hour thinking about Daryl and what he's done to those babies. Just the thought of it makes me want to puke. I pull around back and park alongside the trash bins. As I get out I see the Charger carefully parked behind them on the other side. My nervousness triples at the sight. I pull out the knife before setting out down the path. Surprisingly, my hand is steady and my legs are sure. I can feel my will driving me toward the shed. It's gotten real hot and humid since I left. Summer is definitely here. My shirt's already soaked with sweat by the time I get past the kudzu and into the deep woods. I need to do this before it gets too dark—otherwise, he'll have too much of an advantage. The sky's already turned red, and the tiny fluorescent yellow dots of lightning bugs blink among the trees. It's twilight now.

SPRINTING FULL ON, IT DOESN'T TAKE LONG to reach the clearing. Without slowing down I keep running straight at the shed door and bust in, praying I'm not too late. It happens in an instant. I don't even have time to react. He must have seen me coming through the window because he's waiting for me from beside the doorsill. He grabs my wrist with the quickness of a cobra, and we're spinning around as we struggle for that knife. It's almost like we're ballroom dancing. His blue hat flies off, and his greasy brown hair's all in his face, but I can still see his cold eyes. I try to ram him against the table, anything to jar him, but he keeps pulling away, using my own momentum to keep me off balance. Then he drives us out the door, slamming us both into the ground. The knife comes loose, and for a moment I lose my bearings. It gives Daryl enough time to grab the knife. He stands up real slow, dusting himself off. "Whew," he says. "You almost got me. Next time, try using stealth, dummy. I could hear you trampling here from a mile away." He rubs the knife across his pant leg on both sides and takes a good hard look at it. I get ready to bolt. Then, he smiles and shakes his head. "Whoa. Whoa now. Stay. You've come a long ways. I won't be needing this anyhow." He tosses the knife off to the side. "I knew you'd come," he says. "You always do. Just like that first day. You came for me . . . and them." He takes off his grimy shirt, revealing scars all over a lean, muscular body. "You're a real killer, you know that?" he says.

"Yes, I am," I say. *I've almost caught my breath. Keep talking.*

"What's gotten into you, boy?"

"I'm a killer of the cold. Of the darkness."

"Ha-ha. You've gotten full of yourself since I last seen ya. Shit. One way or another . . ." he says. "If I have to beat you and then use your hands . . ."

Just a little longer, I say to myself. *Keep talking. Give me a little more time to catch my breath.*

"Maybe I'll cut them off."

There's no way I can win in a straight fistfight. He's too strong. He'd kill me. I've got to get close, right up to him. If there's any space between us, I'm done. But I can't let him get on top of me.

"You'll be thanking me"—he keeps talking—"in the end."

I make a run headfirst to tackle him around the waist. He makes a "Hmph!" sound, and we both land on the ground grappling each other. Using his superior strength, he tries to turn us over, but when he does, I pull off and squirm on top of his back. If I could get a rock, I could bash the back of his head in, but he's too fast and there aren't any big rocks. I can't get ahold of him—he's too slippery. So I get my arm around his neck and hold on. He turns us over again, this time with me on my back and him on his back on top of me. He's trying to squeeze me against the ground. But I don't let go.

Then he grabs my wrapped hand, which is at the end of the arm around his neck, and starts squeezing at it with both hands. "Ahhhh!" I yell. I can feel the wounds getting torn open all over again. He realizes going at my wounded hand isn't enough to get me to let go, so he starts rolling like a crocodile rolling its prey underwater. He rolls us all over the ground, trying to get me to let go. He's starting to get desperate. My chokehold's working. He stops rolling around and tries to pry my arm loose, but his hands are weaker than before. They slap at my arm and my face haphazardly. He's squirming now. I can beat him. I *am* beating him. I can barely believe it. I squeeze even harder. The weaker he gets, the stronger I get. This has to end. Then I feel a jolting pain in my ribs. For a moment I think he somehow got the knife and stabbed me. I feel it again and again. He's slamming his elbow into my ribs with everything he's got left. I can't help it. I have to let go. He crawls away coughing and spitting, taking in these deep breaths. *The knife.* He's dragging himself in the direction of where he tossed the knife. I grab him by the waist, but he keeps crawling and kicking me away, like a snake trying to shed its skin. I'm barely holding on by his ankles when there's a loud crack. He stops kicking, and I think, *God, he's got the knife*. I struggle back up to him as fast as I can but he's not fighting back. He's just twitching slightly.

"Samuel! Get away from him," yells Mrs. Greenan from the edge of the clearing. She has a rifle trained on Daryl. I look down, and there's a patch of blood blooming from his side.

"I never thought they'd live this long." He looks sidelong at me as he speaks. He's breathing heavily, kicking up some dust from the ground when he does. "They weren't supposed to live this long. Three months, the doctor said. They're demons. Kill them. Kill—"

"Samuel! Get back!" She's walking up with the muzzle aimed at his head. I sit up on my butt and scoot back. It feels like I've been lifting concrete blocks all day. My arms are shaking really bad. I'm sore all over.

"I brought 'em into this world," says Daryl. "I had to take them out . . ."

Mrs. Greenan is in tears. Her face is all squinted up from crying. She starts yelling at Daryl: "You shouldn't have done it. When you crawled into my bed that night, all sweaty and stinking of whiskey . . . what you did to me, your mother. You're my son. How could you do that? It wasn't right what you did to me. And it ain't right what you're doing now."

"It made me a real man." Then he whispers. "My sons. My brothers." And stares at me with lifeless eyes. I get up and stagger back to the shed, holding my aching ribs with trembling hands. *Don't be dead.* The three boxes sit there lined up evenly on the worktable. I don't want to look inside them, but as I step up to do so, I hear a cough. Down in the corner by the bunk is the skunk bag. I open it, and the babies look up at me in terror. They're real quiet. But then when they see me, they squeak. "Eeeek." And like the first time I saw them, it feels like electricity inside me. But I don't feel like puking or anything like that. It's something else. I grab ahold of them and pull them against me. I can feel their heartbeats, the breath of life coming from those perfect mouths, and the vital movements of those misshapen limbs. Just as human as me. One of them grabs my hair with his good arm, and another has his tiny little hand on my cheek. Then it comes out of one of them. "Momma!" it screams. The other two follow along, screaming "Momma!" In their voice I can hear my own, calling out to a mother I lost and hope to find once again. I feel a gentle hand on my shoulder. I look up to find Mrs. Greenan.

"Oh, thank you, Samuel. Thank you. Your mother would sure be proud of you."

"I'm sorry," I tell her. "I'm sorry."

"There ain't nothing to be sorry about. You saved them. You're a hero."

I hand her two of the babies and hold one myself. We leave the shed. The lifeless body lies on the ground staring up at the sky. All the strength and power it once contained now leaked out into nothing. The black boots look almost childish sprawled that way, the brogans sad and washed out. He looks like a homeless person taking a nap on the ground. "Come on," Mrs. Greenan says. "There ain't nothing to look at here." And we go out onto the path with the babies in hand. After a while the one I'm holding stops crying and holds on to my neck tightly with its one good arm. It looks out ahead of us, and I spend half my time watching it. From the side, its head and face look perfectly normal. The fine and thin hair is wet and matted down around the nape of its neck. I can smell its baby sweat, and it's sweet. I remember that night with Daryl in the house. "I'm sorry," I whisper, moving my mouth silently.

When we get to the end of the clearing, I can see Mrs. Greenan's Oldsmobile parked behind the Charger. She puts them on a blanket in the backseat.

"Go," I say.

"What about you?" she asks.

"There's something I gotta do. Go on home."

She backs out from beside the trash bins and drives back to the front of the Kmart. When she's gone, I hop into the back of the truck. I grab the gas can Jim always keeps back there and toss it onto the ground. I check my pocket for the pack of cigarettes and lighter Jason gave me that night. Then I jump off and grab the can. It's another long walk back to the clearing, especially with that gas can in my left hand. When I get there, Daryl's still lying there dead, quiet. I pour the gasoline all inside the shed, around the whole clearing, saving Daryl for last. Before I pour the gas on him, I slip his wallet out of his back pocket and take out the picture of my mom. I feel stronger just looking at her. I put it back in my wallet behind my driver's license. Then I take that rotten picture he took of me and the babies and lay it on top of him with his wallet and pour out the rest of the gasoline until he's nice and soaked. With the little gas left I make a trail from the shed to Daryl's body all the way back to the path at the end of the clearing. I light it and run, feeling this great weight lifting off of me as I move through the woods. The red on the horizon has been replaced with a deep blue that's already blackening at the zenith of the sky.

I SLIDE INTO THE TRUCK and the smell of Pine Sol mixes with the gasoline from my hands. I roll down the windows before driving to the front parking lot, where I almost run over some kids coming out of the Kmart. As I'm pulling out I look in the rearview mirror and see smoke and even a little red coming from the woods back there. I hit the accelerator and pull out onto the street. It's hard as hell driving like that with my busted hand and the shakes I'm getting. Close to home I pull over and smoke one of the cigarettes to steady myself. I dry heave a couple of times and sit there staring out at the pasture that the road cuts through. It's quiet except for a lone car that passes me. The smell of honeysuckle slowly enters the cab of the truck. I pick up my cell phone and call Melody. She picks up after the fifth ring.

"Hey, there's something I want to tell you," I say. "Something I've been wanting to get off my chest."

"Well, go ahead then," she says kind of coolly.

"I'd like to tell you in person."

"What is it?"

"No, I don't want to say it over the phone."

"Are you in some kind of trouble?"

"No. Just . . . can I tell you something? It's about how I've been acting weird."

After a thoughtful pause she replies, "That I'd like to know. Where are you?"

"On my way home."

"All right. How about I meet you there?"

"Fine. Let's go somewhere else from there, then."

"Whatever. You didn't rob a bank, did you?"

"No. I'll see you soon." I hang up and sit there for a while listening to the crickets and watching it get darker and darker, the red sun sinking lower over the hills and treetops. A bird slowly glides by, barely even having to flap its wings. It's those V-shaped wings that make me believe it's a hawk. I can't remember seeing something so damn nice. By the time I get back on the road homeward bound, the stars have begun to appear in the shallow night sky.

When I pull into our driveway, there's a light on inside the house and Melody's there sitting on the trunk of her Fiat, which is parked behind Dad's car. "C'mon," I say. "Let's go."

"Go where?" she asks.

"I don't know . . . anywhere. Let's just go. We can talk in the truck."

"What's the rush? Anyways, your dad wants to show you something."

"You talked to my dad?" I ask.

"Yeah, he came out and told me to bring you inside to show you something he made. He says you'll know what I'm talking about." Melody's met my dad a few times at the hardware store and at the house, too, but I've always been around. It was strange them talking together without me there.

"Don't worry," I say. "We'll come back."

She leans over into the window and points. "What happened to your hand?"

"Basketball injury, it's nothing. Get in," I say.

"Did you get in a fight?"

"Just get in."

Then Dad comes out from the garage and waves for me to come in. I get out of the truck, and Melody and I walk into the garage. "He was trying to get away," Melody tells Dad.

"He was, was he? How's that hand?" he asks me.

"It's fine."

"Who makes narrow steps without railings?" he says.

"Huh?"

"Jim told me how you fell down the steps at his apartment. I've seen those steps. Whoever designed that place was a fool."

"Right, the steps. I went kersplatt." I look over at Melody to see if she'll say anything about the inconsistency in my story but she just shakes her head.

"Well, did Melody tell you about the project?" Dad asks.

"You're finished."

"That's right. Me and Jim are going to hook up the last part of the wiring. Why don't you wait in the laundry room?" Dad scurries back into the house. He looks like a little kid. I haven't seen him this excited since the Braves went to the World Series. Melody and I go into the laundry room in the back of the garage where there's a door that leads to the backyard. She closes the door and it's pitch-black in there. I can't see a thing.

"Leave the light off," she says. There's a slow hum coming from the water heater. "Now, you want to go ahead and tell me what was on your mind?" her disembodied voice says in the dark. It's almost solemn the way she says it, and it makes me even more compelled to speak.

So I start talking. It's kind of hard at first and I'm kind of mumbling, but soon the words come. "She'd got word about the growth in her head before, but she still had time left. So, my mom and I were supposed to go on some cruise. We hadn't spent that much time together, and she thought it would be good for us. Dad had to work, and Jim had just left for college. It wasn't long or anything, just off the coast of Florida. Three days of going around in circles and coming back to the port. That was it. My mom had got us this package through a travel agency." I wipe my brow thinking there's sweat there, but it's dry. "We met all the other local passengers at the mall, and they were all young, you know." I can feel my lip quivering. "I had packed a small suitcase and somehow it got lost. It had my iPod in it and everything. I got so pissed and blamed my mom. I used it as an excuse not to go, so she went on her own. Dad didn't like it, but I went with some friends to the beach instead. It wasn't even that far from where the cruise ship launched. I didn't want to go because I felt embarrassed because I was with my mom." I swallow a lump in my throat. "She was there all alone on that boat with that tumor in her head"—I cringe—"while I was playing with my friends."

"Samuel," Melody says soothingly.

"After I had my fun I got back home and it was almost like normal, you know. Mom didn't say a word about the trip, but I was nervous all the time. I was just waiting for someone to say what a shit I was, but no one did. It was like that for a couple of weeks. Then she just fell."

"Samuel."

"She stayed in the hospital hooked up to all these machines. It was like she wasn't even human. She just stared into space like a zombie. Almost like a vegetable, except her mouth just moved a little like she was trying to talk without a sound. She was like that for three days, then she died." My face is hot and wet with tears. "I thought I killed her." I catch my breath. "I was the monster. I hated myself. I was the one that I wanted to destroy. Not them. Not anyone else." I hold my face. In the comfort of the dark in that laundry room, in the presence of my confessor. Then Melody places my head on her shoulder. And I feel warm inside. The kind of warmth I felt with Naomi. The kind of warmth I felt from my mom. It stays like that for some time. Then I hear a strange sound. It's like a big machine faltering and then stopping. Then a large *pop* sounds, and the water heater cuts off. It's completely quiet. "What happened?" she asks.

"Sounds like the power went out."

I can hear Dad and Jim coming out of the house into the garage. Melody and I quickly separate from our embrace, and Dad and Jim come in with flashlights. "I told you it was too much juice . . ." Jim's saying.

"I've used a lot more than that, son." Dad turns to Melody and me. "Just a power surge. Just got to flip the circuit breakers."

"Dad, make sure the main line is off before you switch on the one for the outside outlets," says Jim, following behind our dad.

"When'd you start worrying so much?" With the door open there's some light, and I can see Jim and Dad squeezing into the back of the laundry room, in between the water heater and the washing machine where the fuse box is.

Dad opens the box and Jim says, "There's too much power coming in through the outside. Switch the main power off first."

Dad flips a switch and there's another loud *pop*! And then a *zap*! Then the hum of the water heater comes back on. In the darkness I see a small flicker, then a flame seems to come out of the wall where the circuit breakers are.

"Dad!" I yell.

"I can see it!" he yells back and he and Jim start to beat at the flame with their hands wildly like they're trying to kill a scorpion on the wall. "Get it! Get it!" The flame just dances this way and that.

After some more frenzied flailing, the flame has only gotten larger. I quickly open up the washing machine, which is empty. Then the dryer. Inside is a fresh batch of underwear, T-shirts, and towels.

"Here! Smother it!" I say, and toss them some towels. They grab them and smother the flame until it's completely extinguished. Jim and Dad are breathing real heavily.

"Jesus!" says Jim. "That was close."

"Good work, son."

"What? That was about the stupidest thing I've ever seen," says Jim.

"I was talking to Samuel."

"Oh right. Yeah, quick thinking, bro."

The laundry room lights are switched on by Melody. I'm looking at her, and she gets this look on her face and covers her mouth. And I turn to see Dad's thinning gray hair standing straight up and Jim's brown longish hair sticking out in every which way. What's funny is they have no idea. They just have this panicked wide-eyed look about them.

"What is it?" asks Jim. He looks over himself and when he sees Dad, he gets it. "Do I look like that?" They both start laughing when they see each other. I can't remember seeing either one of them laughing like this. It's been a long time. It's the best feeling in the world.

They both feel for their hair. "It must have been the electric charge," says Dad as they get a hold of themselves. "Did you feel it?"

"Yeah, but it just felt like static electricity. Not enough to give me an Afro. I want to see how it looks in the mirror." Dad and Jim squeeze out between the water heater and washing machine. "Why don't you head on out and see the finished product." Dad thumbs toward the backyard. As they leave the laundry room Dad turns off the light and it's dark again in there. Then I see a glow coming from under the door.

"I guess this is it," Melody says, and opens the door to the backyard. I'm struck with an intense brightness. It's coming from those pipes Dad had been planting into the ground. All the plastic pipes put together form a thick white trunk that goes up about six feet high; at the top the ends curve out. I don't think I could even get my arms around it it's so thick. At the top of the curved ends of the pipes he's placed high-powered lightbulbs, the kind used in searchlights, but because of the way the pipe ends were placed and how they are angled, it's like a blossom forming a kind of orb of light that expands out to create a sphere of light covering the entire backyard and the edge of the woods behind it. I walk out into the grass and stroll about, looking up into the branches of the pecan trees in our yard, and I can see little parachutes from when Jim and I used to throw those up there and watch them float down. We had thrown footballs to get them, but three are still dangling from the branches up there. I look at Melody, who's standing by the back porch. With all that pale light illuminating her, she looks like a ghost again, just like that time at the bridge. She smiles and says, "You did get in a fight, didn't you?"

"I fell down some steps."

She shakes her head. "Did you win?"

I answer with a smile. Dad and Jim step out from the sliding doors onto the back porch. Dad has a can of Budweiser in his hands, and Jim has put on a hat. They're smiling, happy. Together. They walk down the steps of the back porch and stand beside Melody, the three of them there on the edge of the illumination.

"I'LL LEAVE THE LIGHT ON FOR YOU, SON," my mom had said.

CHAPTER 21

SUMMER PASSES AS FAST AS A BOLT OF LIGHTNING, and the new school year begins in the fall. A couple of months into school I'm having to take a practice SAT test like everyone else in my grade. An even more rotund and sweaty Principal Reeves wants everyone to get high scores so the school looks good. It's Monday, right after lunch, and I'm out behind the soccer field with David, smoking one of his cigarettes along with him.

"So what made you change your mind about going out for the varsity basketball team?" he asks.

"I'll probably just end up sitting on the bench even if I make the team. But what the hell. I just feel like doing it."

"Looks good on college applications, right?"

"Eh."

"What does Brad always say? It pays to be a dumb jock, right?"

"Right.

We put out our smokes, and I head back into the building. David's ditching the rest of the day to work at the garage. He'll do fine on the SAT without the practice test anyway. So I jog back to the building and catch up to Will and Brad, who are walking down the hallway to the cafeteria talking about how hot Katy got over the summer.

"I bet you she got a boob job."

"No way . . ."

And they go on like that. The hallway's full of disgruntled and confused-looking sophomores carrying their lunch to their homerooms. Some of them complain openly about us juniors doing this to them. All the juniors are taking a practice SAT in the cafeteria, which means the sophomores have to take their lunches back to their homeroom.

"It's not our fault," I say to them as they walk by.

"Yeah, eating outside is good for your health!" adds Will, pounding his chest. "The bracing air, the open space! Breathe it in!" We have a good laugh at that. I don't know why they're complaining, though, I would have preferred eating in my homeroom.

Jacob, an extra-smart sophomore in my advanced algebra class comes walking by, and we all stop. "Take a look at this, Samuel," he says. On his plate is a stack of blueberry pancakes with butter and syrup dripping down the side, along with a side of eggs and sausages. "They ran out of the regular food and only had this left. Does this look like lunch to you?"

"Looks good," I say.

"If it looks so good, then have a bite."

"No, man, with foods like that, it's all or nothing for me. Anyway, I gotta go take that practice SAT." I notice Will eyeing the plate, with some sort of deviousness in mind. "Don't even think about it."

"I wouldn't do that if I were you," says Brad.

Will puts an arm around my shoulder and points at Jacob. "I was going to do it to him, not you, man."

"Like I said, don't even think about it." I push Jacob along and start for my homeroom. "You guys go on ahead," I tell Will and Brad. "I'll meet you in the classroom."

"You're scary," Will says to me with a smile. I shake my head and laugh.

I go to my homeroom and get my number-two pencils. Then I go back to the cafeteria to get back in line for the test. Katy and Debbie are having a last-second look at a preparation book.

"It's too late for that," I say. "You should have done that over the summer."

"Look at you. You look like you want to take this thing," says Debbie.

"I don't want to take it," I say. "I just wanna get it over with." But I feel like hopping around, I'm so excited. The studying I've done over the summer seems like a dream I'm already close to forgetting. We all file into the cafeteria and we're supposed to sit in the order in which we're standing in line, but when the guys around me get to a table, instead of sitting in order, they separate. Will, Brad, Katy, Debbie, and all the rest of my friends sit on one side, and these other kids who are considered not so cool sit on the other end. If I'm to sit in order, I should sit by those other kids, but all my friends are sitting on the other side. I look around the cafeteria. At the far end I see Cornelius and Yoshi sitting with all the black kids. Opposite them is a group of nerdy kids, and at the corner are the artsy hipster types. There're the real poor kids, the super Christians, the rednecks . . . it just keeps going. *Shit*, I think. It isn't anything personal to any of them. I walk across the cafeteria to where Melody's sitting and squeeze in beside her with a good feeling that I can't understand at all.

SPECIAL THANKS TO:

Kathleen, Guan Yin, Yfat, Omma, and Appa,

Jae and Barb, Angie, Bart, Everard, Wes,

Sloane, Karin, Kevin, Kwang Lim, Sarah, Tae,

Mark, Jeanette, Mary Beth, and Hyang Soon.